"I won't say I'm unhappy you're single again."

That was all it took. Desire hit Conner with the force of a head-on collision. He wanted her. Like no other woman before. Wanted her so desperately, he couldn't be trusted alone with her a moment longer.

"It's getting late." He stood, his legs weak at the knees, and removed his jacket from the chair. "I should leave."

"All right." She walked with him to the living room. Before they reached the door, she stopped him with a hand on his arm and a soft "Wait."

"Did I forget something?"

"Only this." She lifted her lips to his and brushed them lightly across his mouth. "I've been wanting to do that all night."

Fire exploded inside him. He dropped his jacket, grabbed her by the shoulders and held her in place against him. "If I kiss you back, I won't stop there."

Dear Reader,

Every story needs an ending, and if you're a lover of romances like I am, you want that ending to be a happy one! I'm thrilled to bring you *Cowboy for Keeps*, the fourth installment in my Mustang Valley series. I realized once I'd finished the third book, *Baby's First Homecoming*, that we still didn't know the origin of Prince, the incredible wild mustang found roaming the McDowell Mountains of Arizona. Well, I just couldn't let that happen.

My hero, Conner Durham, is a different breed of cowboy. Not only is he an incredible horse trainer, he holds two degrees. Brains *and* brawn. How great is that? Like others in this rough economy, Conner lost his management position due to company downsizing. Dallas Sorrenson, the girl who catches his eye, is on her way up in the world. If that weren't tough enough to take, she's pregnant with another man's baby. Conner should walk away, but he can't. And we wouldn't want him to anyway, now, would we?

As in many of my books, I took inspiration from real life for this one. Last year I read a startling news article about an injured horse, and I couldn't get that story out of my mind. I've used bits and pieces from that real-life horse's terrible ordeal in *Cowboy for Keeps*, where Conner and Dallas help to save a badly injured mare and her young offspring.

I hope you enjoy this story. As always, I enjoy hearing from readers. You can contact me at www.cathymcdavid.com.

Warmest wishes,

Cathy McDavid

Cowboy for Keeps

CATHY MCDAVID

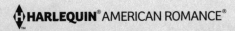

HARLEQUIN® AMERICAN ROMANCE®

Recycling programs
for this product may
not exist in your area.

ISBN-13: 978-0-373-75445-8

COWBOY FOR KEEPS

Copyright © 2013 by Cathy McDavid

Printed in U.S.A.

HARLEQUIN®

™ www.Harlequin.com

ABOUT THE AUTHOR

Cathy makes her home in Scottsdale, Arizona, near the breathtaking McDowell Mountains, where hawks fly overhead, javelina traipse across her front yard and mountain lions occasionally come calling. She embraced the country life at an early age, acquiring her first horse in eighth grade. Dozens of horses followed through the years, along with mules, an obscenely fat donkey, chickens, ducks, goats and a potbellied pig who had her own swimming pool. Nowadays, two spoiled dogs and two spoiled-er cats round out the McDavid pets. Cathy loves contemporary and historical ranch stories and often incorporates her own experiences into her books.

When not writing, Cathy and her family and friends spend as much time as they can at her cabin in the small town of Young. Of course, she takes her laptop with her on the chance inspiration strikes.

Books by Cathy McDavid

HARLEQUIN AMERICAN ROMANCE

*Mustang Valley

To Torno, my first and best horse. You will always run wild and free in my heart.

Chapter One

The tie choked worse than a pair of hands around his neck.

Conner Durham yanked at the knot, loosening the tie, and then ripped it off altogether. He flung the offensive garment onto the passenger seat beside him, where his rumpled suit jacket already lay. The interview, his third with this particular company, had been a complete and utter waste of time.

He wasn't getting the job; the hiring manager had said as much before dismissing him with the dreaded "Thanks, we'll be in touch."

Turning his truck onto the long drive leading to Powell Ranch, Conner slowed his speed to the posted ten miles an hour. He'd have to find a different way to vent his frustration other than pressing his pedal to the metal.

Maybe he'd take Dos Rojo out, work the young gelding in the arena. He and the mustang, named for his distinctive red coloring, were still ironing out the kinks in their relationship, deciding who was in charge. So far, they were even, with Dos Rojo coming out ahead some days, Conner on others.

Driving past the main horse barn, he headed for his quarters, a four-hundred-square-foot efficiency apartment. Hard to believe a mere six months ago he'd owned a five-bedroom house and spent money as if it did indeed grow on trees.

No more, and not again in the foreseeable future, unless his luck drastically changed.

Luck, the lack of it, *had* to be the reason he couldn't find a decent job. It certainly wasn't his qualifications. According to the one-in-twenty prospective employers who'd bothered to contact him after receiving his résumé, he had qualifications coming out his ears. Usually more than the job required.

Little did they know Conner was already downplaying his education and experience in order to make himself more hirable.

Inside the apartment, he swapped the rest of his dress clothes for a well-worn work shirt and jeans. Threading his belt through the loops, he fastened the gold buckle. It was one of his most cherished possessions and proclaimed him Arizona State Champion in steer wrestling. He'd won the buckle in college, before abandoning his cowboy ways in order to earn double MBAs and make his mark in corporate America.

Which he did, for six years, only to fall victim to a massive layoff and departmental downsizing. In the five minutes it took Human Resources to inform Conner that his good pal and fellow manager would take over his position and absorb the few remaining members left on Conner's team, his entire life had changed.

A knock sounding on the door provided a welcome distraction. Another minute and Conner might have started feeling sorry for himself.

Yeah, right. Who was he kidding?

"Door's open," he called, pulling on his boots and standing.

"You decent?" Gavin Powell, Conner's lifelong friend and current boss, barged inside. His glance went straight to the sleeping area, where Conner stood in front of the haphazardly made bed. "Good, you're ready."

"You need something done?"

Instead of answering, Gavin sniffed around the kitchen counter.

"Hungry?"

"I missed lunch. How'd the interview g—"

"Don't ask." Conner strolled into the kitchen, adjusting his Stetson till it fit snugly on his head. "You live in a house full of people. Didn't one of them fix you some food?"

"Sage and the baby are taking a nap, since someone kept us up last night, crying. Dad's down with the flu. Between laundry and helping the girls with their homework, the afternoon got away from me. Do you have any idea how many papers parents are expected to read and sign? Three, just for Isa to go on a field trip."

Last spring, Gavin and Sage had married, joining them and their two daughters, each from a previous relationship, into one big happy family. Now they had a two-month-old son, making their family even bigger and happier.

"Never mind," he complained. "I'll grab some crackers in the office. Which, by the way, is where I need you to be in an hour."

"What's up?"

"I finally hired a photographer. She's meeting with us at four-thirty."

"Us?" Conner quirked a brow.

"You heard right. I need someone to act as a guide. Who knows the story of Prince and is familiar enough with these mountains to lead a day ride. You're the only one I can spare fitting that description."

Conner didn't argue. He owed Gavin for the roof over his head and the food on his table. Literally. If Gavin hadn't rescued him a few months ago, when his severance pay ran out, he might now be living in his truck.

"What about Dos Rojo?" Conner asked. "I want to work him in the arena before the equestrian drill team arrives for their practice."

"Then I guess you'd better get started."

They parted ways on the porch. As Conner crossed the open

area and headed toward the horse barn, the many changes occurring at the ranch during the last two years struck him anew. His own apartment was once a bunkhouse, back in the days when the Powells had owned and operated a thriving cattle business. The smaller of the two horse barns had been expanded to include stud quarters for Prince, the Powells' pride and joy. And the cattle barn, now a mare motel, housed the many horses brought to the ranch to breed with Prince.

Like Conner, Thunder Ranch and the Powells had suffered a grave financial setback, a combination of the economic downturn, loss of their range and encroaching housing developments.

Unlike Conner, the Powells had bounced back, thanks in large part to Prince, a stallion Gavin had discovered roaming free in the nearby McDowell Mountain Preserve. More significant perhaps, the Powells had adapted, turning what remained of their cattle ranch into Scottsdale's most successful public riding stable.

"Hey, boy."

Dos Rojo eyed Conner warily as he approached the stall. The mustang needed an attitude adjustment if he expected to continue living the cushy life of a working ranch horse. Otherwise, he might end up back where he'd come from at the Bureau of Land Management's facility in Show Low, his fate uncertain and, though Conner didn't like thinking about it, possibly doomed.

Not entirely unlike his own fate.

He was determined that the horse remain at Powell Ranch, just as he was determined to find another job.

"Let's go, boy."

They spent forty minutes in the arena, Conner putting Dos Rojo through his paces on a lunge line. When they'd finished, he walked out the horse and gave his coat a good brushing before returning him to his stall. To his delight, Dos Rojo sniffed Conner's hat and nudged his arm as he latched the stall door.

"I agree." He patted the horse's neck. "Good workout. Maybe next time we'll try getting a saddle blanket on you."

There were many things Conner had liked about his former job. The challenges he regularly faced and overcame, the sense of accomplishment, the respect and admiration of his peers and superiors, greeting every new day with purpose.

To be honest, he also found some of those same rewards working for Gavin.

It wasn't enough, however.

The ranch office was located in the barn, beside the tack and storage rooms. As he neared, he could hear voices, Gavin's and a woman's.

Conner's steps faltered, and then stopped altogether. It couldn't be her! He must be mistaken.

The laughter, light and musical, struck a too familiar chord.

His hands involuntarily clenched. Gavin wouldn't blindside him like this. He'd assured Conner weeks ago that Dallas Sorrenson had declined their request to work on the book about Prince due to a schedule conflict. Her wedding, Conner had assumed.

And yet there was no mistaking that laughter, which drifted again through the closed office door.

He contemplated turning around, then thought better of it. Whatever Gavin required of him, he'd do. He owed his friend that much.

Still, a warning would have been nice.

With an arm that suddenly weighed a hundred pounds, he grasped the knob, pushed the door open and entered the office.

Dallas turned immediately and greeted him with a huge smile. The kind of bright, sexy smile that had most men—Conner included—angling for the chance to get near her.

Except she was married, or soon to be married. He couldn't remember the date.

And her husband, or husband-to-be, was Conner's former coworker and pal. The same man who'd taken over Conner's department. Supervised his employees. Expanded his office into Conner's old space.

The man whose life remained perfect while Conner's had taken a nosedive.

"It's so good to see you again!" Dallas came toward him.

He reached out his hand to shake hers. "Hey, Dallas."

She ignored his hand and wound her arms loosely around his neck for a friendly hug. Against his better judgment, Conner folded her in his embrace and drew her close. She smelled like spring flowers and felt like every man's fantasy. Then again, she always had.

Richard was one lucky guy to snare a woman like her.

And, like a fool, Conner had made it easy for him.

She drew slowly back and assessed him in that interested way old friends do after not seeing each other for a while. "How have you been?"

Rather than state the obvious, that he was still looking for a job and just managing to survive, he answered, "Fine. How 'bout yourself?"

"Great."

She looked as happy as she sounded. Flushed—no, glowing, her brown eyes sparkling with curiosity. She'd swept her brunette hair, shorter than when he'd seen her last month, off her face with a colorful band.

Conner could be mistaken, but he thought she might have put on a little weight. It looked good, giving her curves in all the right places.

Married life obviously agreed with her.

"I thought you turned down the photography job." He tried not to stare, dimly aware that he'd interrupted Gavin.

His friend shot him an impatient look. "Like I was saying, Dallas's calendar unexpectedly cleared. She called me last night and volunteered to take the pictures, if we still needed someone, which we do."

She broke out in that incredible smile again.

Conner's heart disregarded his brain's directive and beat triple time.

This had to stop. She was taken, and Conner didn't trespass on another man's territory, even when he disliked the guy.

He needed to get a grip on himself, and fast. How could he expect to work with her otherwise?

The coffee-table-style book, in the planning stages for months, would chronicle the life of Prince, beginning with his capture, to his success as a stud horse, as well as tell the story of the mustang sanctuary, from its inception to today. All profits from the sale of the book would go toward funding the sanctuary and raising awareness of the plight of wild mustangs.

As an avid advocate of no-kill animal shelters, and a professional photographer, Dallas had been the Powells' first choice. It was Conner, in fact, who'd introduced her to them back in the day, when he was on good terms with Richard. Since then, she'd become friends with the Powells, frequently volunteering at the sanctuary. She'd initially agreed to work on the book, but then there had been that conflict.

No more, apparently.

Conner would do whatever was required of him to help the Powells and Clay Duvall, whose rodeo arena currently housed the sanctuary. They weren't just his good friends, he also supported their efforts to rehabilitate former wild mustangs and place them in good homes.

He just wished he didn't have to work with Dallas.

"I thought maybe you two could head out to the sanctuary this morning," Gavin continued, oblivious of the internal battle waging inside Conner. "Get started with some pictures, figure out what all needs doing and how you're going to manage it."

Dallas beamed. "Wonderful idea!"

"I have a class at five." When Conner wasn't overseeing the bucking and roping stock at the Duvall's rodeo arena, he taught riding classes at Powell Ranch and lead trail rides.

"I'll cover for you." Gavin started for the door.

"O…kay." Done deal. Conner was going with Dallas to the sanctuary. "We'll take my truck."

She accompanied him out of the office and to the apartment, where he'd parked.

"I thought you drove a Dodge," she commented, upon seeing his older model Ford.

"Used to." He didn't elaborate, preferring not to advertise that he'd traded in the Dodge, along with his convertible and motorcycle, for a secondhand truck without monthly payments.

"Oh." Understanding registered on Dallas's face. "I'm sorry about your job. Triad Energy Systems lost a good department head."

He opened the door for her. "Guess they kept the better man."

She met his gaze. "They kept the man with more seniority."

Not the kind of remark he'd expect from Richard's better half.

"You'll excuse me if I don't ask how he's doing."

"Actually, I wouldn't know." An indefinable emotion flickered in her eyes. "As of two months ago, we're no longer engaged."

It took several seconds for her words to register, longer for their implication to sink in.

Dallas Sorrenson was not just single, she was available.

CONNER HAD ALWAYS BEEN easy to talk to, his boyish charm encouraging conversation. It wasn't the only quality Dallas had liked about him.

Did like about him.

Talk flowed easily on the ten-minute drive from Powell Ranch to the mustang sanctuary at Duvall Rodeo Arena. Well, with two minor exceptions.

When Dallas inquired after Conner's job search, he gave her one of those nonanswers and promptly changed the subject. They also didn't discuss what had happened between her and Richard, though the news of their breakup had clearly stunned him, requiring a full minute for him to regain his ability to speak.

Not that Dallas blamed Conner for avoiding any discussion of her former fiancé. Richard had been retained and awarded a raise while Conner was let go. He wouldn't be human if he didn't harbor a grudge.

"I always love coming here," she said as they drove past the rodeo arena with its bucking chutes, bleachers and livestock holding pens. A group of men were practicing on their cutting horses, separating calves from a small herd and driving them one by one into a pen. Correction, several men and two women, Dallas observed upon closer inspection.

She wouldn't mind getting pictures of the women. Maybe she'd ask Conner to stop briefly on their way out if the group was still practicing.

"Not too much happening this time of day." Conner aimed the truck onto a long, straight dirt road, at the end of which were the pastures where the mustangs were kept. "If you want some photos of calf roping or bull riding, there should be a decent turnout tonight. Guys practicing for tomorrow's jackpot."

"Will you be working the jackpot?"

"Yeah. I fill in for Clay during events and on weekends. When Gavin doesn't need me."

Despite her curiosity, she didn't pressure Conner for details. Did he enjoy living the cowboy life 24/7 instead of now and then? Prefer it over the manufacturing plant and the constant mental grind? What had happened to his girlfriend, the tall, willowy swimsuit model?

"Sage mentioned you're at the sanctuary almost as much as at Powell Ranch."

He cast her a sideways glance. "You talked to her about me?"

"Only in passing. I was there last week. Taking pictures of the baby." Dallas pressed a hand to her stomach as they went over a pothole.

"How's the documentary photography coming?"

She was surprised he remembered, and flattered. "I'm continuing to pursue it. In between weddings and family reunions and conventions."

Being a commercial photographer was her livelihood but not her passion. She had hopes that the book on Prince and the mustang sanctuary would launch her artistic career. That and the volunteer photography she did for several local no-kill animal shelters.

"Don't forget baby pictures," Conner added.

"Right." She smiled, glad the momentary awkwardness between the two of them had passed. Not only for the sake of the book, which would require them to spend considerable time together during the next few weeks, but also because of her fondness for him.

He was fond of her, too, and attracted to her. Still. Dallas could tell. When they'd first met—she'd been retained by Triad Energy for a company brochure—there were instantaneous sparks. First, they'd gone on a group lunch together. Then a happy-hour gathering after work. Their next happy hour had included just the two of them. It had ended with a kiss that left her thinking of nothing else for days.

By the end of her two-week project, she'd been completely smitten and convinced he had all the potential to be the one.

During that same period of time, Richard had also made his interest in her known. Dallas liked him, but kept him at arm's length, her attention focused entirely on Conner. After her stint at Triad was over, however, he'd stopped calling her so much, then not at all. He cited work and spending weekends at the office as the reason, and apologized. Dallas had believed him. She'd heard the employees talking about a potential large contract and that Conner would be in charge.

After two weeks without a single peep from him, she gave up hope. Richard's call and invitation to a movie wasn't entirely unexpected, and she'd accepted. The rest, as the saying went, was history.

She'd be lying if she didn't admit Richard was a rebound romance. And that she'd occasionally wondered what might have been if Conner hadn't become buried in work.

Well, they were both unattached now.

Dallas instantly dismissed the notion. She couldn't think about seeing anyone right now, and not for a while. She and Richard had only recently split. And then there was the matter of—

"Is this close enough?" Conner asked, interrupting her train of thought.

"Perfect."

He'd pulled the truck alongside the larger of the three connecting pastures, not far from a gate. About a hundred yards off, four mustangs had raised their heads to stare at them. Not completely used to humans, they were content to stay put and watch. That would change as soon as Conner removed the bucket of grain he'd brought along.

Dallas hopped out of the truck, grabbing and then discarding her sweater. It was early October, and, typical for southern Arizona, the seasons were only now starting to change from summer to fall. The mildly nippy early-morning air had warmed as the sun rose. By afternoon, they would be running the air-conditioning in their vehicles.

Standing with the door open, Dallas rifled through her equipment bag, grabbing her digital camera and two lenses, one a zoom on the slim chance the horses proved able to resist the lure of a treat. Depending on the shot, she occasionally used a 35mm camera. A good photographer always allowed for choices.

She met up with Conner at the gate.

"Wait here," he instructed. "These ponies are fresh off the Navajo Reservation and pretty unpredictable. I don't want you getting hurt."

Dallas started to tell him she wasn't a novice where horses were concerned and could handle herself, then reconsidered. Things were different now, and she'd be wise to practice caution. So she did as instructed and waited beside the gate, readying her camera.

Conner shook the bucket. That got the attention of the horses, and they meandered toward him. Dallas raised her camera and studied the scene through the viewfinder.

These mostly untamed horses were perfect for the book, in looks and disposition. Despite their shaggy coats, long manes and tails, and compact muscled bodies, they were extraordinary, and they knew it.

Not just any horse, they carried the blood of their Spanish ancestors, brought over on ships crossing the Atlantic Ocean nearly five hundred years ago. It showed in the proud, regal way they held their heads, the intelligence reflecting in their eyes and the graceful movements of their bodies.

Dallas was transfixed—by the horses and also by Conner.

He might possess two MBAs and be as smart as a rocket scientist, but he belonged to this land every bit as much as these mustangs. How many systems analysts handled a rope as if it was an extension of their arm? Had an uncanny ability to predict a horse's next move? Wore their jeans, Western shirt and cowboy hat with the comfort and ease of a suit?

Conner did.

Except Dallas liked him infinitely better in jeans.

She snapped several pictures of him while he waited for the mustangs to approach, certain he had no idea he was the focal point of all her shots.

A mild breeze tousled the lock of unruly blond hair that swept across his tanned forehead. His hazel eyes narrowed with interest as he studied the approaching horses. A shade shy of six feet, he had the build of an athlete despite spending the last six years in an office, and he carried himself with confidence, completely ignorant of his effect on the opposite sex.

For every hundred or so pictures Dallas took, she might use one for the book. To that end, she snapped away.

"I want to get a few shots of the baby." Without waiting for Conner to reply, she climbed the fence and straddled the top rail, careful to maintain her balance.

The filly, no more than six months old, cooperated nicely, turning her sweet face toward the camera. When Dallas went to climb down the fence, the material of her slacks caught on a piece of wire. She momentarily wobbled and let out a startled yelp.

"Don't move!" In a flash, Conner was at her side, assisting her down.

The horses fidgeted, not entirely happy with this new intruder on their side of the fence.

When both of Dallas's feet were firmly planted on the ground, she looked up and went instantly still. Conner's nearness, not to mention his strong hands resting protectively on her waist, brought a rush of heat to her cheeks.

"Th-thanks. I'm all right."

"You sure?"

No, she wasn't. Sure *or* all right.

"I'm fine. Really," she insisted, silently scolding herself. She wasn't some silly buckle bunny or schoolgirl, and her reaction to Conner was entirely over the top.

He turned from her in that unhurried manner of his. "I was thinking, maybe we could grab a cup of coffee at the Corner Diner when you're done here. Strictly work," he clarified, when she didn't respond. "To go over what you need to do and how we'll accomplish it."

"Of course. Strictly work." She shoved her disappointment aside. Conner was right; they needed to maintain a professional relationship. For many reasons. "Except, if you don't mind, I'd like something a little more substantial. I wasn't feeling like eating earlier, and now I'm starving."

Twenty minutes later, they made their way toward Conner's truck. The ride to Mustang Village, where the diner was located, didn't take long. The uniquely designed, equestrian-friendly community had been constructed on land formerly owned by the Powell family.

Where cattle once roamed, commercial buildings, a retail center, apartments, condos and houses sat. The slow flowing river remained, but the lush vegetation growing on its banks had been replaced by a fence and keep-out signs. Horses still carried their riders across the valley—on bridle paths networking the area, not the open range.

Powell Ranch, four generations strong, looked down on Mustang Village from its place on the mountainside, a witness to the wheels of progress.

"You grew up in this area," Dallas commented as they pulled into the diner's parking lot. "Does it seem strange to you, seeing all the changes?"

"Sometimes." He grinned affably. "When I was twelve, Gavin's dad started letting me go with them on cattle round-ups. The corrals were over there." He pointed to the park a block down the street. "The loading station just beyond them. We'd drive those cows from all over the valley right past this very spot."

"What a sight that must have been." She imagined the pictures she'd have taken. Hundreds of cows on the move. "I bet you loved it."

"Are you kidding? It was dirty and sweaty and backbreaking work."

"You did love it!"

He grinned again. "The only thing more fun was the night we captured Prince."

"You'll have to tell me about it."

"For the book?"

She shook her head. "I'm only responsible for the photographs. I just want to hear any stories you have from the days before Mustang Village was built. For inspiration."

They entered the half-empty restaurant and were promptly seated.

"If I do, you'll fall asleep," Conner said, opening his menu.

"I doubt that. The last thing you are is boring."

He looked up at her.

When their gazes connected, a zing went through Dallas, half warm and pleasant, half...

Wow!

So much for keeping their relationship professional.

Was he feeling it, too? Did he also sometimes think about what might have been?

Attempting to distract herself, she perused the diner's daily specials and waited for her unpredictable stomach to protest. It didn't. Whew. She wasn't going to embarrass herself in front of Conner.

After giving their orders to the waitress, he removed a pen from his shirt pocket and began making notes on a paper napkin. "I was thinking of Saturday for our trip into the mountains. Unless you have plans for the weekend."

"No plans." She peered at the list he was making, tilting her head and reading upside down. Water, snacks, twine, a tarp, a map, GPS, first aid kit, rain ponchos.

"Is eight o'clock too early?" He continued to scribble as he talked.

"No. I'm up at six most days."

"Any preference on a mount?"

"Just something broke. Very broke. Like, if there's a freak earthquake while we're out, the horse won't so much as swish his tail."

Conner's brows drew together. "You're an experienced rider, aren't you?"

"Yes, but I'd rather not take any chances."

"If you're worried about the trails being rugged, we can always take the easier ones."

"It's not that." She set her fork down, suddenly nervous.

"What then?"

She hadn't planned on making any announcements until she started showing.

"Well." She mustered a smile while rubbing her damp palms on her slacks. "I'm pregnant."

Conner spilled several drops of coffee onto the table before managing to steady his mug. "Pregnant! Wha…when?"

"When did I find out? A couple weeks ago. And to answer both questions you're too polite to ask, yes, Richard knows about the baby and no, we didn't discover I was pregnant until after we'd called off the engagement."

Chapter Two

Twice in one morning Dallas had thrown Conner for a loop. First, when she'd told him about her broken engagement. Then the really big bombshell.

She was pregnant. With Richard's baby.

A hundred thoughts raced through Conner's head. First and foremost, there went the possibility of him asking her on a date.

"Do you think it's wise, riding a horse in your condition?"

"The thought occurred to me, too. What if we took ATVs?"

"Motorized vehicles aren't allowed in the preserve." Conner shook his head. "We'll cancel the trip. Gavin can find another photographer."

"I'm doing this. With or without you."

He'd forgotten how stubborn she could be when she set her mind to something.

"I know the book's important to you," he stated.

"Honestly, I don't think you have any idea. Yes, it will educate people on the plight of wild mustangs. And the profits will benefit the sanctuary. But this book has the potential to launch my career. Take it to an entirely new level." She continued in a gentler tone. "It may also be my last opportunity before the baby's born."

"What if you'd fallen off that fence earlier?" Conner asked. "You might have been hurt. Or worse."

"What if you walk in front of a moving car when we leave the diner? There are no guarantees in life."

"And no reason to take foolish chances—which riding a horse when you're pregnant is."

"You said yourself we can take the easy trails."

"Not happening." He could be as stubborn as Dallas. "And don't think you can find someone else. I'll put the word out. Most cowboys in these parts are my friends."

Dallas startled him by reaching across the table for his hand, slipping her fingers easily, naturally, into his. "I appreciate your concern."

Conner stared at their joined hands, unable to tear his gaze away. The rest of what she said dissolved into a jumble of unintelligible words.

Her fingers, with their pink-tipped nails, were delicate and soft as silk. He could imagine them stroking his cheek or caressing his arm. Imagine lifting her hand to his mouth and brushing his lips across her warm, smooth skin.

He suddenly straightened, reason prevailing.

She was pregnant. With Richard's baby.

He should not, under any circumstances, be having these kinds of thoughts about her.

"Please, Conner." Her index finger drew tiny circles on the back of his knuckles. "There isn't anyone else I want to work with on this assignment."

So much for reason prevailing.

Instead of telling her to stop, he prayed she would go on indefinitely.

"Does, um, Gavin know about the baby?" he managed to ask in a hoarse voice.

"No." The tracing of circles abruptly stopped. "I haven't told him."

"Because you're afraid he wouldn't give you the job?"

"I'm only ten weeks along." She withdrew her hand and

squared her shoulders. "I can do this. My pregnancy will not interfere. And if you're considering telling Gavin—"

"I'm not telling him." Conner picked up his coffee mug. It didn't feel anywhere near as nice as Dallas's fingers. The haze surrounding his brain, however, had dissipated. "You are."

"What?"

"Seriously, Dallas. He has a right to know."

"Are you making that a stipulation of working with me?"

"No. I'll take you anywhere you want to go." He'd also do whatever was necessary to protect her.

"Except into the mountains."

"Not until you tell Gavin and he agrees."

"You'll let me ride a horse?"

"Hell, no!" His loud response had several heads swiveling in their direction.

"You just said—"

"We'll take the wagon. Less jarring than on horseback."

Her eyes lit up. "I've never ridden in a wagon before."

"We can't go everywhere we could on horseback."

"What about the canyon where you captured Prince?"

"I'll check the maps, verify the trails. We might have to take a longer route, but we'll get there."

She sat back, a satisfied and most appealing grin on her face. "Thank you, Conner."

"Promise you'll let me know if the going gets too rough."

"I will."

"I'm serious."

"Taskmaster." Her brown eyes sparked with delight.

"You have no idea."

"Right."

Clearly, she saw straight though him. The last thing Conner would do was push her, physically or emotionally.

"We'll find Gavin when we get back to Powell Ranch."

Dallas made a face. "I have to tell him today?"

"It will take me a while to ready the wagon and the team of horses. I'm not starting until he gives me the okay. The ranch is liable, after all."

"You going to make me get a note from my doctor, too?"

"That's not a bad idea."

Dallas grumbled, then dived into her remaining salad, polishing it off in a few bites, along with the rest of her meal.

Conner watched, forgetting about his coffee. Did all pregnant women inhale their food? He hadn't paid much attention to Sage and Caitlin's eating habits during their pregnancies.

"I'm not keeping you from your work?" Dallas asked when the last bit of sandwich had disappeared.

"You heard Gavin. You are my work for the next few weeks."

"Good." Rising from the table, she smiled seductively.

Conner waited a moment before snatching the tab and following her to the front of the restaurant, his legs alarmingly unsteady.

Had she just flirted with him?

No, he must be mistaken. Dallas was always that way, friendly and outgoing, with a thousand-watt personality. It was the reason men found her so attractive, Conner included.

Only his interest in her went well beyond casual.

He reminded himself yet again of her current condition and the man responsible for it. Acting on his attraction would surely result in trouble. And until Conner's life was back on track, trouble was the last thing he needed.

THE FRONT DOOR OPENED even before Dallas came to a complete stop in the driveway. Her mother stepped onto the porch and raised a slender arm in greeting, the folds of her vibrantly colored peasant skirt hugging her legs. Gold bangles on her wrists and neck glinted, catching the last rays of a disappearing sun.

The bohemian style of dress was much like the woman herself, free-spirited and uninhibited.

Dallas grabbed the casserole dish off the passenger seat, fussing with the loose foil covering it. Purse in tow and dinner contribution secure, she climbed out of her Prius Hybrid and headed toward the house.

"You're early." Marina Camponella stood waiting with open arms.

Dallas leaned in and let her mother hug her, the most she could manage with the load she carried. "Mom, you look great."

"Thank you, dear." Marina accepted the compliment as she did most things in life: graciously and humbly. "How are you feeling? Any morning sickness?"

"It comes and goes, generally without me having to run to the nearest bathroom. For which I'm grateful."

"Be happy. Morning sickness is the sign of a healthy baby." She gave Dallas's stomach a quick pat and relieved her of the casserole dish.

They went through the tastefully appointed living room on their way to the kitchen. Many of the exquisite pieces on display had been crafted by her mother. A talented sculptress, she'd abandoned a promising artistic career to marry Dallas's stepfather, Hank, and raise her two children.

She still sculpted for personal enjoyment, completing only two or three pieces a year. Teaching at the Horizon School of Art in Tempe took up most of her time.

Glimpsing her newest piece reminded Dallas that her mother wasn't enjoying the fulfilling life she might have if Hank had encouraged rather than discouraged her dreams.

Speaking of which…

"Where's Hank?" Dallas asked, draping her jacket over a kitchen chair and stowing her purse on the counter.

"In the den. Watching the presidential address on TV."

"Ah." Dallas rolled her eyes. "I should have guessed."

"You know Hank and his politics." Her mother opened the oven, and the aroma of baking chicken immediately filled the air.

Curry chicken, Dallas could tell. So could her stomach, which roiled at the prospect of any spicy food.

"I do know Hank," she mused aloud.

How could she not? She'd spent twelve years living under the same roof with him. Arguing with him, disobeying him, rebelling against him and finally just tolerating him until the day she could move out. It wasn't that she hated Hank. Not at all. They were simply polar opposites.

Dallas took after her unconventional mother, something her conservative financial-advisor stepfather didn't understand. If he had, he wouldn't have established such strict rules for two teenagers simply eager to get their feet wet in a big, wide world.

Real-life blended families, Dallas had concluded, weren't like the ones portrayed on TV. They didn't always, well, blend. Dallas's younger brother held a similar opinion and had left home the year after she did.

"Heard from Liam recently?" she asked.

"He's in Colorado. Mapping a remote part of the national forest."

"Sounds exciting."

Liam had also inherited their mother's free-spiritedness. Dallas wasn't sure he'd ever trade his job as a surveyor for a permanent address.

Like her brother, Dallas valued her independence, but she also longed for stability. A husband and children. She believed all things were possible with the right person.

For the last two years, she had assumed that person was Richard. Except then they'd called it quits.

Dallas's mother handed her a stack of plates from the cupboard. "You mind setting the table?"

"Of course not."

She didn't wait for the next item, fetching glasses and flatware while her mom sliced a loaf of freshly baked bread.

"Hank," Marina called, then sighed with exasperation. "He can't hear me over the TV."

"I'll get him." Dallas made her way to the den, following the sound of what had to be a news commentator recapping the address. "Hi, Hank," she said, stepping into the decidedly masculine room, the only one not decorated by her mother. "Mom sent me to tell you dinner's ready."

"Hey." He pushed himself up from the recliner, turned off the TV with the remote control. "I didn't hear the doorbell ring."

"Mom met me outside."

"She loves it when you come to dinner."

Dallas detected a hint of reproach in his voice. As if she didn't already know her visits were too infrequent.

"Work's piled up lately."

"You need your rest." Hank placed a large hand on her shoulder, the gesture more stilted than affectionate.

It was, Dallas had long ago accepted, the best he could manage.

"Have you heard from Richard lately?" Hank asked as they entered the kitchen.

He was fit and tall, and the gray at his temples gave him a distinguished appearance. Dallas could see how her mother had become enamored with him.

"He called Tuesday."

"Today's Friday."

"And?"

"I just thought he might check on you more often."

Dallas automatically tensed. "Why would he?"

Her mother sent Hank a let-it-go warning.

He didn't heed it. "You're pregnant."

Dallas poured iced herbal tea from a pitcher. "I'm only in my first trimester. It's not like there's much change day to day."

"I'd think, as the father, he'd be more concerned."

"Richard's plenty concerned,"

Dallas sat across from her mother, who gave her a he'll-run-out-of-steam-soon head bobble in reply. Marina could conduct entire conversations without speaking a single word.

"He is." Hank harrumphed in agreement. "Concerned enough to make an honest woman of you and give his child his name."

"We're not getting married."

The moment Richard had learned about Dallas's pregnancy, he'd proposed. Or reproposed, in this case. She'd declined. Her parents had married solely because Marina was pregnant with Dallas—not for love.

"You could do worse than Richard."

Dallas bit down, swallowed her retort. She'd come here for dinner, not to argue with her stepfather.

"Hank cares about you, honey," Dallas's mother said in an attempt to smooth things over. "After all, your pregnancy is nothing short of a minor miracle."

"I was supposed to have trouble conceiving, Mom, not carrying."

"And yet you did conceive. Without any trouble." Her face radiated joy. "When you first told us you had PID, I was so sure you were in for a tough road. And then so grateful Richard was willing to brave it with you."

"He was willing because it meant postponing starting a family. His job came first with him."

"He wanted to wait until he was financially secure." Hank helped himself to a serving of chicken. "I think that shows responsibility."

"And you had your budding photography business to consider," her mother added.

A bout with appendicitis in college had left Dallas with pelvic inflammatory disease. Because of scarring on her fallopian tubes, she was told she'd likely require the assistance of a fertility doctor in order to conceive. Finding out she was pregnant couldn't have come as a bigger shock, to her, her family and Richard.

Terminating her pregnancy or giving her child up for adoption weren't options. Dallas was having the family she wanted, simply a little ahead of schedule. And without a husband. Or a house. Or having become a successful documentary photographer.

A knot formed in her middle.

"You should give him another chance," Hank said.

Her mother nodded thoughtfully. "Try living together instead of rushing into marriage."

"We were engaged over a year without ever setting a date. Our instincts were telling us we didn't have what it takes for a successful marriage. A baby doesn't change that."

Dallas was feeling ganged up on. Her mother was fond of Richard and Hank thought there wasn't a better guy out there.

"But Richard is thrilled about becoming a father," Marina gushed. "It would be nice for his sake if you could work things out."

Dallas sighed. It was past time to level with her mother and stepfather.

"I hate to break it to you, but Richard isn't thrilled."

"What?" Her mother gasped. "But he… You said—"

"I didn't want to upset you." Dallas buttered a piece of bread, but she'd lost her appetite. "He wants to marry me because he believes it's the right thing to do."

"He loves you."

"He did. Once." Not for a while.

"I'll talk to him," Hank interjected.

"You will not! I mean it, Hank."

"Someone needs to set him straight."

"That's not your job."

He looked hurt, and Dallas instantly regretted the harsh tone she'd used.

"Are you sure he just doesn't need more time to adjust?" Marina asked, always the mediator.

"I'm asking for you and Hank to respect my wishes and let me handle Richard my own way. Now, please, can we change the subject?"

Awkward silence followed, until Marina chimed in with "How's the book coming?"

"Great. I got some nice pictures of a mustang family at the sanctuary yesterday. Conner took me."

"Conner Durham?" Her mother visibly perked up. She and Hank had met Conner before, during various cookouts and holiday gatherings. "Richard's friend who was laid off?"

"Yeah. He's working for the Powells and the Duvalls, splitting his time between the two places, from what he told me."

"They need a systems analyst?" Hank's brows furrowed.

"Hardly." Dallas laughed. "He's teaching riding classes, supervising trail rides, overseeing the rodeo livestock and managing the mustang sanctuary."

"Such a shame he lost his job," her mother commiserated.

"Richard felt terrible. It ended their friendship."

"Not Richard's fault the economy tanked," Hank muttered. "Sometimes management has to make tough decisions."

"It's not Conner's fault, either. But he's the one out of a job and living in an apartment on Powell Ranch."

"Apartment?" Marina looked perplexed. "What happened to his house?"

"He still owns it. From what Sage Powell told me, he's renting it out to cover the mortgage payment, except the monthly rent isn't enough, and he has to make up the difference."

"That's terrible. It's such a beautiful house."

Dallas remembered visiting it. Five bedrooms, three bathrooms, game room, three-car garage, a pool and a beautifully landscaped backyard. Living in the apartment must be a huge adjustment for Conner.

"He'll move back into the house as soon as he finds a new job."

"Positions like the one he had are few and far between," Hank said. "And the competition is ruthless these days."

Inspiration sprang suddenly to Dallas's mind. "Maybe one of your clients has a job opening."

"Possibly. Let me make some calls on Monday."

"That's really nice of you."

"When are you seeing him next?"

"Tomorrow. We're taking a trip into the mountains to view some of Prince's old stomping grounds."

"Honey, is that wise?"

"Don't worry, Mom. We're taking the wagon, which is much safer than riding horses. I'll be fine."

"I don't know...."

"Trust me. Conner has seen to every precaution."

Marina marginally relaxed. "There's a reason I always liked him. Be sure and tell him I said hello. And call me the second you come down off the mountain. I'll worry."

Dallas smiled. "I love you, too."

She was convinced the trip would be uneventful, other than her getting a lot of shots for the book.

Dinner progressed comfortably and was soon over. "Let me help you clean the kitchen, Mom. I can't stay long. I have an early morning."

"You sound excited."

"I am. Great weather, fantastic scenery, fresh air. It'll be fun."

"Having Conner for company all day will be fun, too." Her mother winked, another nonverbal communication that Dallas pretended to miss.

She didn't like admitting she'd been entertaining the exact same thought.

Chapter Three

"Easy does it, girls." Conner walked behind the pair of fully harnessed draft horses, the long reins gripped firmly in his hands. Because the team was well broke and used to being hitched to a wagon, he was able to accomplish alone what might normally require two men. "Come on," he coaxed. "Almost there."

Molly, the older of the pair, eased into position on the left side of the wagon tongue. Her partner, Dolly, suddenly started veering the wrong way.

"Haw, haw," Conner hollered, using the command to go left.

Dolly obeyed and promptly changed direction, the chains on her harness rattling like the ghost of Christmas past's.

Molly watched, head bobbing and tail swishing. When both horses were lined up, Conner called out, "Whoa," and let up on the reins.

"Need a hand?"

He glanced over his shoulder at the sound of Gavin's approach. "You can help me hitch them to the wagon."

While Conner attached the neck yoke to the collars, Gavin hooked the trace chains to the doubletree.

"You seen Ethan this morning?"

"Earlier," Conner answered. "He called to say he was heading over to the rodeo arena. Clay's new bull is arriving."

Like Conner, Gavin's younger brother worked for their friend Clay. And like Gavin, Ethan had recently added to his family, when his wife, Caitlin, gave birth to a baby girl.

Conner thought about Dallas being pregnant. Just about all of his married friends seemed to be having babies lately.

Except Dallas wasn't married to Richard, and he and Conner were no longer friends.

Checking the britchens and back straps one last time, he tied the mares to the hitching post. Eager to get started, Dolly pawed the ground with her heavy hoof.

Gavin came around the wagon to Conner's side, stopping briefly to unlatch and lower the tailgate. "Maybe you should wait for Ethan to get back before you and Dallas leave."

"What for?"

"He's the expert and could go with you in case there's a problem."

"I know enough about wagons and driving a team to manage."

"Just a suggestion." Gavin shrugged. "Or I can take her."

"*I'm* taking Dallas." Conner dropped the ice chest he'd packed into the wagon bed, shoving it beneath the seat. "My job, as I recall."

"No need to get riled."

"I'm not." He tossed the rain ponchos and rope behind the ice chest.

"You're throwing things around for the heck of it?"

Okay, so maybe he was a little riled at the prospect of Ethan or Gavin replacing him.

"Ask her out," Gavin said.

That halted Conner in his tracks. "On a date?"

"Yeah, on a date."

"You can't be serious."

Together Conner and Gavin loaded several bales of hay

into the rear of the wagon. The extra weight would provide needed balance on the steep hills.

"Why not? You're both single. You like each other. If you hadn't let her slip through your fingers when you did, you two might still be together."

Would they? It was possible. Conner did like her. More than he should. As good of pals as he and Richard were, he'd always been a little jealous of his friend and mad at himself for letting Richard steal her.

"No." Conner all but barked out the word and wiped his damp brow with the sleeve of his jacket. "Not happening."

"Because she's pregnant?" Dallas had told Gavin about her condition and, after checking with his wife and sister-in-law, he'd reluctantly agreed to let her go on the ride into the mountains.

"I don't care that she's pregnant."

"Didn't think so, because your old girlfriend had a little girl and that didn't bother you."

It hadn't bothered Conner. He'd gotten along well with the child and missed her. More than he did her mother, who'd dumped him when his severance pay ran out and he could no longer afford her expensive tastes.

"Be a big step, getting involved with a woman carrying another man's baby." Gavin's voice was absent of judgment.

Conner paused and rested his arm on the side of the wagon. "It's not her pregnancy stopping me."

"Her ex-fiancé? Kind of awkward with him still in the picture."

"No fooling."

Gavin scratched behind his ear. "I'd be wondering if she was comparing me to him."

Conner's stomach clenched. He hadn't considered that unpleasant possibility.

"'Course, there would be a certain satisfaction in dating her. Paybacks are hell."

Conner rarely got mad, but his temper abruptly flared. "If I was to ever go out with Dallas, and I'm not, it wouldn't be to get back at Richard. She's too good for that."

Gavin chuckled and retreated a step. "Hey, relax. I wasn't serious."

Conner reached for the canvas satchel containing the snacks he'd packed, shoving it next to the ice chest.

Gavin watched him closely. "What's the real reason you won't ask her out?"

"Richard being her baby's father isn't enough of one?"

"I know you, buddy, and you've got a hankering for Dallas. Did from the first time you laid eyes on her."

Conner wished his friend was less astute.

He had always been drawn to her. She was pretty and genuinely nice, with a heart of gold. Her small, curvy body enticed him more than his model-thin ex-girlfriend's ever did.

What really appealed to him, however, was her gumption. Her adventurous nature and love of life. Her many passions and her dedication to them. The fearless way she pursued her ambitions.

Conner had been the same once. Passionate and fearless, with an endless supply of gumption.

Then he'd lost his job and a large chunk of his self-esteem in the face of countless thanks-but-no-thankses.

"Richard was a fool to let her go."

"Here's your chance, buddy," Gavin continued. "You don't ask her out, I guarantee you someone else will, pregnant or not."

"I'm not asking her out," Conner repeated.

"She doesn't care that you aren't bringing home six figures a year."

He jerked at the reminder of his former circumstances. "I care."

"Money's not important to her."

"Easy to say." Conner's ex-girlfriend used to profess a similar sentiment. Funny how people change.

A horn beeped, causing both men to turn. Dallas waved from her Prius, then headed behind the barn, where the parking area was located.

"You're wrong." Conner returned to loading the wagon. "A husband who can provide for her and her child is what's important to her."

"She tell you that?" Gavin asked.

"It's what she deserves." And what, at the moment, Conner couldn't give her.

"She's planning on raising her child alone. If money was important to her, she'd have stayed with Richard."

"He's paying child support, or will. On his salary, it ought to be plenty generous."

"Ah," Gavin said knowingly.

"What does that mean?"

"If your ego was any bigger, it'd swallow you whole."

Conner glanced at Dallas, who was quickly approaching and almost within earshot. "This has nothing to do with my ego."

"Right." Gavin let loose another chuckle.

Connor cursed under his breath. Once again, his friend's insightfulness was right on the mark.

THEY ENTERED the mountains at one of the trailheads behind Powell Ranch. For the first twenty minutes, Dallas could hardly sit still. Head swiveling, she took in the view from her elevated vantage point on the wagon seat.

"Nice."

"You haven't seen anything yet."

They reached the first hill and began their ascent. Conner clucked to the horses, which leaned into the harness as they pulled their heavy load.

Dallas swallowed. "This is steeper than I thought it would be."

"You want to turn back?"

She dug her fingers into the seat. "Absolutely not!"

The trail, barely wide enough to accommodate the wagon, curved sharply. Conner guided the team of horses, talking to them in a calming tone.

Dallas told herself he'd promised they'd take the easy routes, and she trusted him.

That was until she looked down.

No one had warned her how different riding in a wagon was from sitting astride a horse. How much higher it was.

Large boulders flanked the trail, close enough to clip a wheel. If that happened, they'd career over the edge. And what an edge it was. On the other side of the boulders, the ground gave way, ending far below in an overgrown gully.

Perhaps she should have given more consideration to this day trip.

"Pretty, huh?" Conner asked.

"Very." When she didn't look down.

"You'll appreciate the view even more when we get to the top."

"How, um, reliable is this brake?" She ran her hand over the smooth handle, finding comfort in its nearness.

Conner's hardy chuckle allayed some of Dallas's worries

"You don't have anything to worry about. Once we crest the top, it's all downhill from there."

"Until the next one."

"True. But the second half of the trip is mostly flat," he added.

She let out a sigh of relief.

"And here I always figured you for having nerves of steel."

"I do have nerves of steel." She lifted her chin. "If I didn't, I wouldn't be here. I'm just more comfortable when I'm in the driver's seat."

"You want to take over for a while?" He started to pass her the reins.

She shook her head. "You're doing great."

"Seriously, if you want to try driving awhile, you can. When we reach flat ground and the girls are tired out. Less chance of a runaway then."

Her fingers clenched the wagon seat tighter. "What exactly are our chances of a runaway?"

"Almost none." He turned to face her. "Do you think Gavin and Ethan would have given all those people rides around the park during the Holly Daze Festival last Christmas if they thought for one second they'd have a runaway?"

"I guess not."

Conner stared at her. At her mouth. Then his gaze traveled to her eyes, where it stayed…and stayed. "I wouldn't do anything to put you in danger."

She melted, inside and out, and let go of the wagon seat.

"That wasn't so hard, was it?" he asked.

"No." She could, she thought, go anywhere with him. "What was it like?" she asked after a moment. "Capturing Prince."

"Not easy, I can tell you that. He's a wily one and gave us a run for our money. Took six of us to herd him into a corner and get a rope around his neck."

"What did you think when you first saw him?"

"That I'd met my match. I'd never worked with a wild horse before, much less rounded one up and brought him in."

"And now you work with wild horses every day." Too late, Dallas realized her slip. He hadn't worked with horses every day, wild or otherwise, until he'd lost his job. Before then, it had been restricted to weekends.

If her remark bothered him, he hid it well. "Only until they're trained. Which doesn't usually take long."

"You are good at it. You could train horses for a living if you wanted." Shoot, another stupid slip. Would she ever learn? "Not that you aren't a great systems analyst."

Ugh! That sounded worse.

"Ethan's the resident horse trainer on Powell Ranch. I wouldn't want to take his job away from him."

Like Richard had taken Conner's job.

"I, um, was just—"

"It's okay, Dallas. You don't have to walk on eggshells. I got laid off. Now I'm training horses and leading trail rides, and glad to have a job. Plenty of the people I worked with at Triad Energy still don't."

"Something's going to break for you soon. I have faith."

"Glad one of us does."

"It's all about networking," she said enthusiastically.

"So I've heard." His grin strived for teasing—and fell short. Had she overstepped?

Dallas kept quiet rather than commit another blunder.

Conner broke the silence first. "Do you mind if I ask a personal question? You don't have to answer if you don't want to."

"I don't mind."

"Why did you break up with Richard?"

She took a moment to collect her thoughts. "Technically, it was mutual."

"It still must have hurt."

"Not really. Which says a lot. I took it in stride. Sure, I was a little lost at first. But by the end of the following week, I was ready to move on. Which says even more."

"What happened? Between you."

"Nothing happened, which was the problem. Whatever we had, it wasn't head-over-heels, can't-live-without-you love."

"When did you find out you were pregnant?"

"A week later."

Conner nodded, watched the trail ahead as it grew steeper and steeper.

Her curiosity got the best of her. "What are you thinking?"

"I'm surprised you didn't change your mind and decide to get married, after all. Richard has his faults, but he's a responsible guy."

"If you must know, he did ask me."

"Hmm."

"I said no. Nothing's changed."

"Except you're having his baby."

"Which hasn't affected my feelings for him. I care for him, I really do. And I imagine I always will. But not enough to marry him."

"You could do worse."

Dallas stiffened. Now Conner sounded like Hank.

"My mother spent five years married to a man she didn't love. He wound up walking out on her and my brother and me. It sucked, and it's the last thing I'd want for my child. Given a choice, I'd rather call off the wedding than go through with it, only to wind up divorced a few years later."

"Sounds like you're justifying the breakup."

She scowled at him. "I am not."

"A father has a duty to fulfill."

"My father? Or are you referring to Richard? Forget it," she said, before Conner could answer. "Richard will do his duty. We just won't be married."

"I admire you. It's a big risk you're taking. Most women would be scared."

"I'm scared, all right. Petrified. But I have the support of my family and friends. And my work. Photography is something I can continue while I'm pregnant, and after the baby's born."

He made a face.

"What?" she demanded.

"You'd bring a baby along on a wagon ride?"

"Not all my shoots are in the mountains."

"Or from three thousand feet up?"

He'd remembered the photos she took last year that now appeared in a calendar. "Guess I won't be hot-air ballooning for a while, either."

He was right. Her entire life would soon be completely different.

Was she making the right decisions for everyone concerned? Most important, her baby?

She and Conner reached the top of the hill. He drew the horses to a stop so they could rest.

Dallas had lived in the Scottsdale area her entire life and considered herself familiar with the landscape, having photographed it countless times. Even so, the view sent a rush of awe coursing through her.

"Cool, huh?" Conner grinned as if he'd discovered this view himself.

"Way cool." Without thinking, she bent and reached for her camera bag on the floorboard beneath their feet. The strap evaded her grasp, and she had to abandon her efforts. "Is it possible for us to get out? I'd love some shots."

"No problem. The girls could use a rest."

He reached around her and set the brake. Gripping her hand, he steadied her as she climbed down the side of the wagon. Only when she was safely afoot did he wrap the reins around the handle and descend. Dolly and Molly didn't budge, except to give each other a disinterested sniff.

While Dallas clicked away, Conner waited beside the horses, gripping Molly's bridle.

"You were right. The view is amazing." Dallas was already mentally composing the list of contacts she'd send the photos to in the hopes of making a sale.

Conner materialized beside her. "Watch you don't get too close to the edge." He took her elbow, drew her back a step.

A step that brought her up close and personal with him. *Tall. Broad. Strong. Masculine.* The words blinked in her mind like a flashing neon sign. Conner was all those things and more.

"I'll be careful," she assured him. Careful to keep a watch on her heart. He could easily steal it.

She returned to the wagon bed and reached in the ice chest for a bottle of water. What she really needed was space. No reason to put ideas in either of their heads.

Dallas might be over Richard, but she was still vulnerable. She didn't need a man messing with her priorities. Derailing her plans.

She'd seen the results of that firsthand with her mother.

Moving to a different spot, she continued snapping pictures. The mountains, harsh and primitive, erupted from the earth like an offering to the heavens. At their base, the city, with all its modern wonders, spread out in every direction, devouring the landscape.

These were the kind of photographs Dallas sought, the ones that told a story.

Conner appeared in her viewfinder, unaware that the camera had found him. He stood staring at the city. Behind him, a rocky brown ridge rose like a wall. Cacti and shrubs grew out of it, clinging to existence against impossible odds.

Molly, her head beside Conner's, also stared at the city, with a look of ancient wisdom in her eyes.

It was as if the past and present were colliding right there in front of Dallas.

Talk about a story.

Chills ran up her arms as she snapped a quick shot. Then a half dozen more. Instinct told her these would be her best pictures of the day.

"You done?" Conner asked.

"I am." God, she loved her work.

The drive to the box canyon took another hour and a half, during which Dallas and Conner chatted amiably.

In the canyon, he tethered the horses to a tree and then fetched water for them from a natural spring. They drank lustily, emptying one bucketful after another.

Dallas unloaded the ice chest, adding the trail mix and protein bars she'd brought to Conner's canned tuna fish, crackers and apples. It was, in her opinion, a perfect lunch.

Afterward, they walked the length of the box canyon. He watched over her as she got all the pictures she needed and then some. Several shots included him, but none were as compelling as the ones from the top of that first hill.

When they finally pulled out, about two o'clock, Dallas's eyelids were drooping. Sleeping was impossible with the wagon bumping noisily along the narrow trail.

"Thanks again for taking me today," she said.

"My pleasure."

Hers, too.

"Can you imagine what it must have been like, crossing the country in a wagon? How incredibly tough those people were to have endured the hardships they did."

Her comment sparked a lively discussion about pioneers heading west, which eventually segued into one about the history of Mustang Valley. Before Dallas knew it, they were ascending the first of the large hills.

She scanned the horizon, always on the lookout for more photo ops. All at once, a metallic twang sounded, like a coiled spring being released.

Conner glanced down and swore, then yanked on the reins. "Whoa, girls." To Dallas, he said, "Pull the brake."

"What's wrong?" She responded to the urgency in his voice, her fingers grabbing for the brake handle as a spear of alarm sliced through her.

Chapter Four

Once the draft horses were at a standstill, Conner peered over the side of the wagon and assessed the damage. He didn't like what he saw.

In a matter of seconds, the entire flat iron tire had separated, remaining attached to the wheel by a single bolt.

"Conner?" The concern in Dallas's voice reminded him that he hadn't answered her question.

"We've damaged a wheel." He reached behind her and checked the brake, making sure it was set firmly. Handing her the reins, he started to climb down. "Stay put."

"Wait!" She perched on the edge of the seat. "What if the horses bolt? I'm not sure I can hold them back."

"They won't bolt." He threaded the reins through her fingers. "Just keep a steady hold on these."

Dolly and Molly waited patiently, though holding the heavy wagon on an uphill grade couldn't be easy.

"You sure?"

"I need you to stay calm." He reached up and rested a hand on her shin. "The only reason these horses would run off is to get away from your squealing."

"I'm not squealing," she insisted, doing precisely that.

"Right." Conner hid a grin as he squatted beside the wagon to examine the damaged wheel.

"How bad is it?"

"The tire came off."

"I thought wagons had wheels."

He touched the dangling band of metal. "This is called a flat iron tire. It protects the wood."

She scooted to the edge of the seat and angled her head for a better look. "Can you just take it off?"

"I could try, but we wouldn't get far before damaging the wheel beyond repair. Then we'd really be stuck, and Gavin would have to come after us with a truck and trailer."

"What are we going to do?"

"Call for backup." He removed his phone from his belt and checked the reception, which could be hit-or-miss in the mountains. "Have Gavin bring us a drill and spare bolts so we can repair the tire enough to make it home."

When he powered up his phone, the screen flashed No Service. "Dammit," he muttered. Served him right for changing to a cheaper carrier. "Where's your phone?"

Dallas looked stricken. "In my purse. Locked in my car. I didn't think it would work up here, so I didn't bother bringing it."

He scanned the area, debated his options. "I'll walk up the hill. Should have better reception up there. But first…"

Seeing what he needed, he set out on foot.

"Where are you going?" Dallas stared over her shoulder at him, her grip on the reins viselike.

"Not far." Collecting two large rocks, he wedged them tightly behind the rear wagon wheels. He quickly located two more rocks and did the same with the front wheels. The extra precaution should prevent the wagon from rolling backward until they were rescued.

Next, he began unhitching the horses.

"Should I get down now?"

"Sit still. Keep hold of the reins until I tell you it's okay." She grimaced nervously but complied.

Conner hurried.

"Good job, girls," he said, unhooking the last chain and giving Molly's rump a pat. He returned to Dallas, who was more than happy to relinquish the reins.

He watched her every move as she climbed down, ready to grab her if she slipped.

It turned out Dallas was nimble as a monkey. On the ground, she swiped her hands together with a job-well-done flourish. "Need any help?"

"I'm good."

"Too bad we didn't bring along a spare saddle and bridle. We could have ridden out."

"I'd have rather brought a toolbox. I won't make that mistake again."

Conner led the horses to a tree, the largest in the vicinity, and tied them securely. "Be right back," he said, and headed in the direction of the hilltop.

"Can I come with you?" Dallas chased after him.

"Better stay. Someone has to watch the wagon and horses."

"If that wagon rolls backward, I won't be much help."

"You can holler. I'll come running."

"By then it will be too late."

"Would you rather call Gavin? He'll need directions on where to find us. And a list of what tools to bring."

"I won't be much help with that, either." She shrugged. "I have no clue where we are."

He brushed a tousled lock of hair from her face. Her skin was cool to the touch and incredibly soft. "It's going to be fine. The worse that will happen is we're late for dinner."

Possibly really late if he didn't get through to Gavin.

He'd be stuck with Dallas. For hours. Maybe all night. They'd have to cuddle in the wagon under the tarp to stay warm.

"I, um—" he cleared his suddenly dry throat "—I'd better get going."

Her fingers clutched his jacket sleeve, delaying him. "I'm sorry to be such a wimp."

"It's okay to be scared."

"I'm not scared." She lifted her face to his. "Not with you."

He was sure she could read his every thought, sense his every emotion.

Warning bells went off inside Conner's head, creating an enormous din. He moved quickly away before temptation won out and he crossed the line into dangerous territory.

HALFWAY TO THE TOP, Conner glanced back at Dallas. She'd perched on a large boulder not far from the wagon, hugging her knees. Was she thinking of him? Of those moments that kept occurring between them?

He was.

Impatient, he dug out his phone. One bar appeared in the corner. Enough to try.

The signal took forever to connect, the icon blinking endlessly. Frustrated, Conner hit the end-call button and tried again. Finally, Gavin answered.

"Conner, what's up?"

"We have a problem."

"You there? I can barely hear you, buddy."

Sharp static cut off every third word. Conner strode farther up the hill. "Is this better?"

"Some."

Speaking loudly, he quickly summarized their predicament.

"We'll take the ATVs," Gavin told him. "It'll be quicker than riding. I doubt the Forest Service will give us grief for using them, since it's an emergency."

Before Conner finished with the details of their location, he lost the connection. Moving to a new spot made no difference. He blamed the clouds, which had drifted to gather overhead.

Not rain clouds, fortunately. Tomorrow, however, would be a different story, according to the weather report.

He could only hope he'd relayed enough information to Gavin for him to find them. In their favor, no one else in these parts knew the McDowell Mountains better than his friend.

Dallas hopped to her feet at Conner's approach, relief written all over her face. "I heard you talking to someone."

"Gavin's on his way." Conner decided not to worry her about the incomplete directions. "My guess is he'll bring one or two guys with him."

"How soon till they get here?" She rubbed her arms through the material of her thin jacket.

"An hour. Two at the most. Are you cold?"

"Not yet." She peered anxiously at the clouds.

"I brought the rain ponchos. They're also good for conserving body heat."

"That may come in handy if Gavin's late." She reached over the side of the wagon for the ice chest and opened the lid. "Right now, I'm thirsty." She removed two bottles of water. "Want one?"

"How comfortable is that boulder?" Conner downed half his bottle.

"Not very."

"There's a nice spot over there." He indicated a place near the horses. "We can sit while we wait for Gavin."

Her mouth turned down at the corners. "Looks a little rocky."

"I can fix that." Conner stepped around her, gripped the edge of the wagon seat and pushed up. It immediately came loose.

Dallas gasped. "You mean to tell me that thing's not nailed down? What if it had come off during the ride?"

Conner removed the seat and set it on the ground. "We'd

have had to be going over a pretty big bump at a full gallop for that to happen."

She didn't look reassured.

"Come on." He carried the wagon seat to the spot he'd chosen and set it down, making sure it was stable. "Ladies first," he said, gesturing grandly.

Playing along, she gave a little curtsy before sitting. "Thank you, sir."

He joined her, the seat bouncing on its spindly legs.

The location was a good one. It allowed them an unobstructed view of the trail, the wagon, the horses and the city.

"What are the chances someone will come riding by?" Dallas asked.

"Not much. This isn't the most popular route."

"I should get my camera." Dallas's gaze wandered. "Could be worse. At least the scenery's beautiful."

Conner studied her profile. "It sure is."

"I know that's South Mountain, and over there's Camelback." She pointed to a craggy range in the far distance. "Which mountains are those?"

"The White Tanks," he answered, without taking his eyes off her face.

"Incredible," she breathed. "We can see the entire valley from here."

She must have become aware of his scrutiny because she turned to face him. "Do you even know where I was pointing?"

"Yes."

Laughter bubbled out of her, lively and enchanting.

If not for his mouth having gone completely dry, he'd have joined her.

Was she the least bit aware of her effect on him?

"I had dinner at my parents' last night."

She was distracting him with small talk.

"How are they?"

"Good.

"I bet your mom's happy about the baby."

"Are you kidding? She's ecstatic. Already making plans. Has a furniture maker friend building a cradle and an artist friend designing a mural for the nursery wall. She said to tell you hello, by the way."

"Give her my regards." The wagon seat creaked in protest as Conner shifted. There wasn't much room, and their thighs inadvertently brushed, then their elbows.

Dallas didn't seem to mind. Conner sure didn't.

"Hank mentioned he may have some clients who are hiring. He's going to make some calls tomorrow."

Conner's defenses rose. He hated the idea of Dallas and her family discussing his lack of employment. "I don't want to impose on him."

"It's no trouble."

Conner didn't need help. Not from Dallas or her family. He was more than capable of finding a job on his own. "Since when did I become dinner conversation?"

"I was telling them about our trip today, and they asked how you were."

"I see." He leaned forward and struck a closed fist on his knee.

Dallas must have realized all was not well. "Did I do something wrong?" She placed a hand on his arm.

Her tenderness and compassion could be his undoing if he let it.

"I'm not one to take handouts from people." He had enough trouble with Gavin and Clay. At least he could repay their generosity with hard work.

"Hank calling some of his clients isn't a handout. He's being nice."

She was right. Conner was letting that damnable pride of

his get in the way. Instead, he should be exploring every opportunity regardless of the source.

"Thanks." He covered her hand, which still rested on his arm. "I like that you're thinking of me."

"It's only fair, after all the help you're giving me."

"You really think the book can boost your career?"

"I hope so." A wistfulness came over her. "Someday, my photos are going to be hanging right there alongside Dorothea Lange's."

"Who's that?"

Dallas gawked at him in disbelief. "Only the most influential documentary photographer of the twentieth century."

"Oh, her."

She rolled her eyes.

"I thought your commercial business was doing well."

"It is. Pays the bills. Keeps me busy and out of trouble."

"But you want more."

"What can I say? I crave fame and success. You understand."

He did. The success part, anyway. He also understood how reaching for the stars could result in a spectacular fall.

"Mostly, I want people to look at my pictures and do more than say isn't that nice." The wistfulness from earlier returned. "I want them to get goose bumps. Be inspired. Moved to tears. Have their perspectives changed. Heck, maybe even their lives."

"Wow."

"I know it's a lot." Her cheeks reddened. "And I sound like an egomaniac."

"No, I'm just…impressed. And jealous."

"Of what?"

"You're lucky to be so passionate about your job. Most of us head off to the office, put in our eight hours and head home."

"Didn't you have that kind of passion when you were at Triad?"

He nodded. "I figured on a promotion every few years and staying put till I retired. I never thought for one second it would end like it did."

"Or that Richard would take over your job?"

"That, either." He tamped down the anger that still hovered just beneath the surface.

"You must hate him," she said sympathetically.

"Not hate."

"Despise?"

"I held a grudge. *Hold* a grudge, don't get me wrong. But I'm not angry at him. Not over the company-wide downsizing and his promotion." Conner rubbed his closed fist on his thigh. "He's also trying to do right by you and the baby, and I respect that."

"You think I should marry him?"

"I think you should consider it. Seriously. He can take good care of both of you. Provide a financially stable life."

Unlike Conner.

"What about love?"

"You said yourself you'll always care for him. And you loved him once. Enough to get engaged."

"I think I was enamored with the idea of being in love. And vulnerable at the time."

Because of him? Conner was hesitant to ask, not sure how he'd respond if she answered yes.

"Richard was everything I thought I was looking for then." She stared forlornly at the horizon." I've been unfair to him, and I won't compound it by marrying for the wrong reason."

Conner saw her point. But he'd been raised by parents who instilled traditional values in him. "Richard's trying to do the honorable thing. You might be happier than you think you'll be."

"Two horses." As Conner spoke, the pair emerged fully into view.

The larger one, a mare, was flanked closely by a youngster, no more than six or eight months old by the size of him. The pair progressed cautiously up the hill toward Dolly and Molly, heads bobbing, the colt's dainty legs dancing.

"Are they wild mustangs? Like Prince?" Dallas watched in amazement.

"That would be too much of a coincidence." Even so, Conner entertained the possibility. He and Dallas crept forward, edging alongside the wagon. "Careful, we don't want to scare them."

The mare, a sturdy tan-and-gray Appaloosa, had eyes only for Dolly and Molly. As she neared, Conner spotted something wrong, something that caused his blood to run ice-cold and his anger to burn.

"What's that in her neck?" Dallas asked. "A stick?"

"An arrow. And there's a second one imbedded in her back."

Chapter Five

Dallas needed her camera. Right away, before the mare and colt ran off. Making as little noise as possible, she reached over the side of the wagon for her bag, and then crept forward.

"Wait," Conner instructed in a low voice. "She looks tame. Let's see if I can get her to come to me."

"And if she doesn't?" Dallas whispered back. "I want pictures. To show people."

He gave her an arch look.

"This is cruelty to animals," she insisted. "Whoever did it needs to be punished. Pictures can be used as evidence."

"We have to catch the mare first. Even then, I doubt the authorities will find the culprit. It probably happened weeks ago."

Weeks ago? That poor animal.

Conner rummaged around the wagon bed and removed a coiled rope. "When, and only when, I tell you, bring this to me."

Dallas took the rope and stayed put, although she would rather have gone with Conner.

What sane person would shoot an innocent horse with a bow and arrows? The thought made her heart constrict. Fortunately, the colt, a miniature version of his mother, appeared uninjured. Small consolation. If his mother died—infections could linger—he'd be left to fend for himself, with practically no chance of survival.

Good thing she and Conner had come along when they did, and that the wagon wheel had broken.

The mare gave Dallas and Conner only a cursory glance. She instead fixated on Dolly and Molly, who fidgeted nervously and tugged on their lead ropes.

Dallas wasn't sure if the draft horses wanted to be friends with the newcomers or run from them. The colt was also undecided and pranced skittishly in circles around his mother, while eyeing Conner warily. Had he ever encountered humans before?

Excitement coursed through Dallas. The colt, she realized, must have been born here in the mountains. Like Prince!

Slinging the coiled rope over her shoulder, she removed her camera from the bag, one eye fastened on Conner.

Rather than continue toward the mare and colt, he changed direction and headed instead to Dolly and Molly.

"What are you doing?" Dallas asked in a loud whisper.

He held out a hand, indicating for her to be quiet.

Impatience clawed at her. What if the mare and colt ran off before she got a decent shot? Ignoring Conner's directive, she inched out in front of the wagon and began taking pictures.

A moment later Conner reached Molly and untied her lead rope. His intention became evident when he began walking with her back to the wagon. He was trying to see if the mare and colt would follow.

Capturing the pair might turn out to be a simple as leading them home.

Dallas gave Conner credit for his ingenuity, and then admired it as the mare broke into a trot to catch up with Molly. The colt bucked twice for good measure before loping alongside the mare, his slender legs moving gracefully.

Conner's grin conveyed his satisfaction with the outcome.

Dallas deftly switched to a zoom lens. Appalled at the unspeakable and senseless cruelty of some people, she forced herself to keep snapping shots.

"Bring the rope," Conner said.

She stopped shooting and did as he requested. "Oh, dear God," she murmured, upon witnessing the mare's wounds up close and without a camera lens filtering her view. "She must be in terrible pain."

"Bad, isn't it?"

One arrow was imbedded in the muscles of her neck and stuck straight out at a ninety degree angle. The other one had completely pierced the flesh of her back, six or so inches behind her withers. Red and yellow feathers protruded from one end, a bladed arrowhead from the other.

Dried blood the color of tar stained the mare's hide near both wounds, and traveled in a drip pattern down the entire length of her right shoulder and leg. The darkened flesh surrounding the puncture wounds curled away, leaving gaping, abscessed holes.

"You okay?" Conner's voice had an odd, tinny quality to it.

"Fine." Only Dallas wasn't fine. The ground rippled under her feet, and her vision dimmed.

She'd fainted only once before, as a teenager when she had her wisdom teeth removed, but she remembered the sensation well.

"You don't look fine." He supported her elbow.

"Pregnant, is all." She fought for control, barely winning the battle.

"Easy now," Conner said, using the same coaxing tone he did when talking to the horses.

She saw now why they responded to him.

Accepting the support he offered, she leaned on him until the dizziness passed and her head cleared. "I feel stupid."

"Don't. Gives me another reason to hold you."

Was he joking?

"What about the mare and colt?"

"Right here. I don't think she's going to give us any trouble."

"Good. She needs treatment." Steadier and stronger, Dallas edged away from Conner. "I'm better now. Thanks."

"Anytime."

When he offered her a smile, her insides fluttered.

They really should stop flirting and holding each other if they expected to maintain a strictly professional relationship.

Who was she kidding? Their strictly professional relationship had gone by the wayside the moment his lips grazed hers. Probably sooner than that.

"You should tie up that mare before she changes her mind."

Conner nodded, his hazel eyes lingering on Dallas.

Enough already, she told herself. She couldn't continue this—whatever it was with Conner—any longer. She was pregnant and not in the market for a man. Certainly not until she'd determined how, exactly, she was going to continue working while raising her baby as a single mother.

And any man she did choose wouldn't have had his job taken from him by her baby's father.

Conner might find her attractive now, but that would change the moment she started to show. Every time he looked at her, he'd be reminded of Richard.

"You mind holding Molly? If you're up to it." He passed her the mare's lead rope.

"I'm up to it." Dallas was glad to help. And glad for something to distract her from her thoughts about Conner, what they'd once had and what they possibly could have again.

"If she gives you any trouble," he said, "just let go of the rope."

"She won't." Dallas rubbed Molly's nose. The big horse snorted lustily before nudging Dallas's hand in a bid for more petting. "See?"

Dolly, still tied to the tree branch, had lost interest and was dozing, the deerfly buzzing near her head going unnoticed.

Conner turned toward the injured mare. Amazingly, she'd remained where she was, not far from Molly. "Here, girl." He approached slowly, the rope held at his side.

The mare stared at him, her gaze a mixture of curiosity and trepidation. She might have been raised by humans, but she didn't trust them unconditionally. Her colt stood behind her large, round rump, head peeking out. If not for the instinct to stay with his dam, he'd have scampered off a long time ago.

"That's it." Conner took another step.

Dallas suddenly remembered her camera. Stuffing Molly's lead in the crook of her arm, she started snapping pictures, grateful that there was still enough light.

How could she have forgotten to take pictures?

Simple. Conner.

He held out his hand, palm up. The mare arched her neck, sniffed him and jerked back, before sniffing again. Eventually, to Dallas's surprise and delight, she let Conner stroke the side of her face. Another couple dozen pictures were saved to her camera's memory card.

Murmuring to the mare the entire time, Conner lifted the rope, letting her sniff it before uncoiling it one loop at a time.

"That's right," he crooned. "You know what this is, and you want to go home. Had your fill of the hard life, I bet."

Dallas got another shot of Conner and the mare, this one with the arrow in her neck prominent.

He had just laid the rope over the mare's neck, well beneath the wound site, when the low rumble of an engine sounded in the distance. No, two engines, Dallas thought, peering at the top of the hill and listening intently.

Their rescue party was arriving, and none too soon.

Wrong. It was too soon, as a glance at Conner confirmed. He hadn't completely secured the rope, and when the mare tossed her head, it slipped off. She backed away, lowering her head and baring her teeth.

The colt, Dallas suddenly realized. The mare wanted to protect her baby from danger.

Dallas jumped as the first ATV crested the hill and came to a stop, the engine whining as it idled. When the driver—it was Gavin; she could see that now—started toward them, the mare twisted sideways and galloped down the hill, her colt in hot pursuit. Seconds later, they disappeared behind the bend, the clatter of their hooves fading to silence.

"Conner!" Dallas called, but it was pointless. There was nothing he could do, no way he could go after them on foot.

She wanted to cry. Without proper medical treatment, the mare had little, if any, chance of recovery.

"We have to go after them!"

"We will," Conner assured Dallas. He'd just finished telling Gavin and Ethan about the injured mare and her colt. "Just not now. It'll be dark soon. And the ATVs will only scare her away. We'll come back later. On horseback."

"When?"

"Soon." Conner looked at Gavin, who confirmed the plan with a nod.

"Tomorrow?"

"More likely the day after."

Conner had an interview early Monday morning. Though he didn't have much hope of landing the job—the hiring manager had indicated there were several excellent candidates being considered—he wanted to spend Sunday afternoon preparing. Clean shirt. Suit pressed. Fresh copies of his résumé and references. MapQuest directions to the location printed out.

"Can I come, too?" Dallas pleaded.

"Sorry. No riding, remember?"

Her hand went to her tummy.

"Speaking of getting dark…" Ethan had removed the tool-box from where it was strapped onto the back of his ATV. "We'd better fix this wagon wheel while there's still some light."

The three men worked well together. Being the one with the most experience, Ethan supervised. It was like old times. The only one missing was Clay. During their childhood, and later as teenagers, the four of them had been inseparable and the bonds they formed unbreakable.

At least, Conner had thought they were unbreakable.

Eleven years ago, after Gavin and Ethan's mother died due to complications from a heart transplant, a feud had developed between Clay's father and Wayne Powell, Gavin and Ethan's dad. Having to choose, and hating it, Conner had sided with the Powells. It seemed to everyone at the time that Clay's father was in the wrong. Nonetheless, Conner kept in occasional contact with Clay, unable to cut his friend out of his life entirely.

As with most disagreements, there was more to the story than met the eye. Last fall, after Sierra Powell returned to Mustang Valley, the truth had emerged. The two families were at last able to put their differences aside and restore their friendship. Good thing, too. If not, the church would have been pretty empty when Sierra married Clay. Instead, it overflowed with friends and family and celebration.

Dallas had also attended the wedding, taking photographs for the bride and groom, as she had at the Powell double wedding, when Ethan and Gavin had married their spouses. Conner had assumed the next wedding she attended would be her own.

He'd been wrong and had yet to decide if he was sorry. As much as he didn't like thinking about Dallas and Richard, their child deserved the best from both parents.

Dallas hovered near the wagon, watching the men. They

weren't progressing as fast as Conner would like. Dolly and Molly shared a similar opinion. Undoubtedly hungry and thirsty, they'd been anxious the last half hour, shifting from side to side and taking periodic nips at each other.

"Do you think the mare and colt are wild mustangs, too?" Dallas asked Gavin. "Like Prince?"

"I doubt it," Gavin said, his voice straining as he and Conner lifted one end of the wagon so that Ethan could slowly spin the wheel and check the flat iron tire. "They most likely escaped from some ranch."

"Hunting is allowed in these mountains?"

"No," he grunted, lowering the wagon when Ethan gave the okay. "This is an urban preserve."

"Then what would somebody be doing with a bow and arrows?"

"Breaking the law." Conner started collecting the tools. "Or she may have been shot near the river, where hunting is allowed."

"That's a long way to travel." Dallas stared at the distant landscape as if she could see the river.

"Take about a week. And her wounds are at least that old."

"Just because hunting's not allowed," Ethan said, "doesn't mean someone wasn't poaching."

"Poaching!" Dallas retreated a step. "That's illegal."

"People break laws all the time."

"Do they also mistake a horse for a deer?"

"Not usually."

"Exactly. Whoever shot that horse was being intentionally malicious."

"She could have been trespassing on a rancher's land, and he shot her."

Dallas gaped at Conner. "To kill her?"

"Chase her off."

"That's inhuman." Her voice rose with outrage. "He could have called…whoever it is you call, and had her removed."

"We're only guessing. Who knows what really happened to her? It might have been an accident."

"Yeah. Two arrows *accidentally* found their way into her neck and back."

Conner noticed Dallas shivering. Unbuttoning his jacket, he said, "Here. Take this."

"I'm all right."

"You don't need to be getting sick."

"I have a better idea," Ethan said. "The wheel's almost fixed. Gavin and I don't need your help to finish." He turned toward Conner. "The keys are in the ATV. Why don't the two of you head on home? I'll drive the wagon and Gavin can ride ahead of me on the other ATV."

"Sounds good," Conner agreed. "I'll come back as soon as I drop Dallas off at the ranch. You should be well on the way to finishing by then."

"I can stay," Dallas protested.

"Don't be stubborn. It's been a long day. You're cold and tired."

"You are, too."

"But I'm not pregnant." He refastened his jacket and unearthed one of the rain ponchos from the wagon bed. "You'll need this. For a windbreaker."

When she didn't budge, he put an arm around her shoulders—and was immediately reminded of holding her during their near kiss earlier.

Lucky Gavin and Ethan hadn't shown up then. He could easily guess what would have gone through his friends' minds.

Given the curious glances they were directing at him and Dallas, their suspicions were already aroused.

He removed his arm.

That didn't stop the stares.

"Come on, Dallas. Think of the baby."

"All right, all right." Relenting at last, she grabbed her camera bag and the rain poncho and stomped off toward the ATV.

Conner sat down first. She straddled the seat behind him, adjusting her camera bag and encircling his waist with her arms. He tried not to notice how nice she felt pressed against him.

"Call my cell if you have any problems." Conner started the engine. "Reception's better at the top of the hill."

"Will do," Gavin hollered back.

"If it gets too cold for you," Conner said to Dallas as they crested the rise, "let me know."

"Don't worry about me."

As if he could *not* worry about her.

What had taken an hour by wagon required only fifteen minutes by ATV. He had to admit she was a trouper, enduring the harrowing night ride without complaint. He drove the ATV right up to where her car was parked behind the barn, and pulled to a stop.

She got off first, peeled away the rain poncho and dug in her zippered jacket pocket for her car keys. "Thanks for everything you did today." The headlights flashed when she activated the automatic door lock.

"Been better if the wagon wheel hadn't broken."

"I'm just glad it was at the end of the ride and not the beginning." She opened her car door.

"Dallas. Wait a minute."

"If you're thinking about trying to kiss me again—"

"I'm not." He paused. "Okay, I am."

She smiled.

"But I'm not going to act on it."

"Probably wise."

Was that a flash of disappointment he saw in her eyes? He must be wrong. The light was playing tricks on him.

"We should talk," he said.

"We should. But not tonight."

With a hand on her wrist, Conner stopped her from slipping in behind the steering wheel. "We can't ignore what happened."

"I don't intend to." She sighed and met his gaze. "How could I? If the mare hadn't interrupted us, I'd have kissed you. And I'm pretty sure I'd have liked it."

Conner couldn't help himself, and grinned—foolishly, he was sure.

"We'll talk," she said resolutely. "In a few days or a week. I'm just not ready to tonight."

"Dallas—"

"Please. I get it. You and I, we're walking through a series of land mines. I'm fresh from a two-year relationship. I'm pregnant. And my ex-fiancé took your job. It couldn't get more complicated."

She didn't add that Conner was struggling financially and had yet to find a decent job. Two more land mines.

"Have a good night, Dallas." Ignoring everything they'd just agreed on, he leaned in and gave her a chaste peck on the cheek. So much for maintaining a strictly professional relationship. She didn't pull away. "I'll call you tomorrow. Let you know what the authorities say about the mare and colt."

"Thanks." She climbed into her car.

He stood back and waited. The engine didn't turn over right away, grinding once, then twice. He was about to suggest she pop the hood when the engine suddenly caught and roared to life.

The moment her car disappeared around the corner of the barn, Conner got back on the ATV. He didn't drive up the trail to join Gavin and Ethan, he practically flew.

He'd kissed Dallas Sorrenson. Again! He might regret it later, but right now, he was pretty damn happy.

Chapter Six

"Thanks, Sage. Dinner was delicious." Dallas rubbed her full stomach. "If I keep eating like I have lately, I'll be as fat as a house soon."

"Enjoy yourself. Being pregnant is one of the few times in your life you get to indulge. Then it's back to dieting. I still can't fit into my prebaby jeans."

Gavin's gaze took in his wife from head to toe, the look in his eyes that of a man who appreciated what he saw.

Dallas wondered if Richard ever looked at her that same way, with such unabashed longing. She thought not.

Conner did. She'd seen him when he thought her attention was elsewhere. Just as she feared she looked at him.

"I'll help you with the dishes," she said, when Sage collected the nearly empty lasagna pan and rose from the table.

"Nonsense. That's the girls' job. Right, girls? You can show Gavin and Conner the pictures you brought once we clear this mess away."

On cue, Gavin's daughter, Cassie, and Sage's daughter, Isa, pushed away from their chairs and scooped up more dishes from the table, obedient but not excited about the prospect of fulfilling their nightly chore. Cassie's faithful companion, Blue, a happy-go-lucky cattle dog, jumped up from his place beneath her chair and trailed after her.

At thirteen, she was poised for transformation from girlhood to womanhood, and eagerly anticipating high school in the fall. She'd talked of little else during dinner. Free from typical teenage drama, she was patient with her seven-year-old stepsister and clearly enraptured with her brand-new baby brother, who was currently enjoying the attention of "Uncle" Conner.

Dallas observed the pair as unobtrusively as possible while retrieving her portfolio from the counter.

Who'd have thought it? Conner was a natural with babies.

He cradled little Emilio, or Milo, as everyone called him, close to his chest. The baby, bathed, dressed in pajamas and swathed in a cotton blanket, resembled a miniature mummy. He cooed and gurgled contentedly, perhaps because he heard Conner's heart beating.

"Milo looks happy," Dallas observed.

"He definitely has a preference for Conner." Gavin wore a half serious, half joking expression on his face.

Conner beamed broadly. "That's because I'm better looking than you."

"Don't listen to him." Sage patted Gavin's shoulder. "He's just had more practice with babies than you."

"Practice? You?" Dallas blurted, before catching herself. Did Conner have a child she didn't know about?

"It's been a while, but my two sisters are a lot younger than me. Fifteen and thirteen years. I was the only guy in high school who could dribble a basketball with one hand and bottle feed a baby with the other."

"You didn't mind babysitting?" Dallas was intrigued. Conner had mentioned sisters before, but she hadn't realized they were significantly younger than him.

"It was torture. At first." His cocky grin softened to a warm smile. "Then I got kind of used to the little rug rats." He gave Milo's chin a tickle.

"He whined like a girl when he went off to college." Gavin snorted. "Missed his sisters more than he did his friends."

"I did not."

Conner took the dig in stride, which made Dallas think that maybe he had shed a tear or two at being separated from his siblings.

"Do you see them much?" she asked.

"Whenever I can."

"Every free weekend," Sage clarified.

Just when Dallas had convinced herself she could stay away from Conner and the potential for more kisses—even chaste ones like last night—he had to go and show her another incredibly sweet and touching side.

He liked babies and was good with them.

He might even like her baby, too.

No. No, no, no. This had to stop. Contemplating any kind of relationship while she was pregnant with Richard's child was simply out of the question.

Opening the portfolio, she withdrew several dozen of the best photos from her and Conner's trip into the mountains, having spent the afternoon getting them developed and enlarged. She hadn't wanted to arrive at dinner empty-handed.

The photo on top was one of the many including Conner.

He'd called her late last night to let her know that he, Gavin and Ethan had arrived safely home with the wagon. Other than Dolly and Molly being spent, all went well. She'd suspected the men were also spent.

As she'd requested, there was no discussion of their kiss—the close call on the hill or the peck on her cheek at her car. Instead, their conversation had been brief, impersonal and to the point. She blamed exhaustion. Then decided Conner, like her, was having second, third and fourth thoughts.

His conduct toward her today had been that of a family friend and business associate. What it *should* be.

Why, then, was she disappointed?

"These are the ones of the box canyon and the ride there." Returning to her chair, she started with the pictures for the book, fanning them out in front of Conner and Gavin.

"Here, let me have Milo." Sage relieved Conner of the baby, who emitted a gurgle of protest at losing his comfy roost. "First a bottle, then bed."

"See ya, buddy." Conner gently tweaked Milo's toe through the blanket. "You ever find yourself hankering for a night out with the boys, come see me."

"Conner Durham," Sage admonished, shielding Milo with her body, "you try and corrupt my son before he's full grown, and I'll have your hide. I swear." She fired Gavin a warning look, as well. "You, too, buster."

Conner and Gavin exchanged conspiratorial glances.

"I saw that!" She huffed, and then addressed Dallas. "If you want, you can rock him to sleep when you're finished here. Practice for when you have your own baby."

Dallas was filled with sudden warmth. "I'd love that. Thanks."

"You two finish your homework when you're done with the dishes," Sage instructed the girls. "No TV till then."

"I need help studying my spelling words." Isa had tucked a dish towel in the waistband of her jeans to serve as an apron.

Just like Cassie, Dallas noticed, and smiled.

"I'll help you," Gavin said.

"Cassie, can *you* help me?" Isa pleaded. "Please?"

"Sure, squirt." She tousled Isa's hair.

"Humph." Gavin looked displeased. "I think I've just been insulted."

Isa came over and gave Gavin's neck a hug. "You're the best riding teacher, but Cassie's better at spelling."

He patted her cheek. "All right. If you put it that way."

"These are good." Conner had been sorting through the pictures, picking up first one and then another.

"They are," Gavin concurred. "Going to be hard choosing only a few for the book."

When their favorites had been determined and set aside, Dallas showed Gavin and Conner the pictures of the mare and colt. Even after examining the images repeatedly throughout the day, she was shocked yet again—by the extent of the mare's injuries and the savage cruelty of whoever had shot her.

"Sage called her boss at home earlier," Gavin said. "Told him about the mare and baby."

"What did he say?" It being Sunday, Dallas hadn't expected any progress until Monday at the soonest.

"He's going to contact both the Forest Service and the Scottsdale police as well as the deputy director at the Game and Fish."

There was a lot to be said for having connections. After a four-month maternity leave, Sage had just returned to work as a field agent for the Game and Fish Department.

"According to him," Gavin continued, "possibly all three authorities have jurisdiction in the Sonoran Preserve."

"What about capturing the mare and colt? Will they send someone?"

"The Forest Service is going to notify the rangers in the area. Advise them to be on the lookout."

"That's not much."

"It's all they've got. For now. They don't have either the manpower or the resources to chase down loose horses in the preserve. Neither do the police, especially when it's likely the mare and colt will wander off or go back to where they came from."

"What about the Game and Fish?"

Gavin shrugged. "The wheels move slowly."

"But you'll go after them, right?" she asked.

"We discussed that today." Conner leaned back in his chair. "It's a long shot. The preserve is nine thousand acres and the horses could be anywhere."

"You just said—"

"We'll give it a try. Business comes first, however."

"I understand." Dallas didn't quite know why she cared so much about the mare and colt and their welfare. Perhaps becoming a mother herself had something to do with it. "How can I help?"

"Send the photographs to every newspaper and TV station in town. Pressure them into running the story."

"I'll also speak to the head of the Arizona Animal Welfare Association." Dallas was acquainted with him through her volunteer work at the no-kill shelters. "He may have some ideas. And influence with the media," she added, "if I don't get anywhere. With luck, someone knows who shot the mare and will turn them in."

"I wouldn't hold my breath," Conner said. "But we may find her owner."

"I can also print up flyers. Distribute them to the ranches and residential communities located in the foothills." Her enthusiasm grew as the ideas took shape. "The mare's friendly. She'll probably seek out other horses. People, too. If they can't capture her and the colt, they can report their location to us."

Dallas hadn't hesitated including herself.

"It's worth a try," Gavin concurred.

"I'm riding out tomorrow afternoon." Conner fingered the edge of one particularly gruesome picture. "With Ethan and Javier. Clay's willing to help, too, and can spare a few men."

"That's great!" Dallas's gaze went from Conner to Gavin. "Thank you."

"I figured if we didn't help, you'd hound us relentlessly."

"And you'd be right." She began assembling the pictures

on the table. "If you want to keep any or all of these, go right ahead. I have copies, print and digital, at home."

"I'd like that," Gavin said. "I'm sure Sage and the girls want to see them."

"I have one for you." She reached in her portfolio and withdrew the striking photograph of Conner and Molly standing on the hill, the city sprawled below them, the mountains behind them. "It came out really good."

"Hmm." Conner's brows rose as he studied the photograph. "Let me see."

He tilted the picture toward Gavin.

"Nice. Impressive. You going to send it out?" he asked Dallas.

"I have a client or two who might be interested." She reached into the portfolio for a release form and a pen. "Any chance I can get you to sign this?"

Conner passed the photo to Gavin and took the form. "You really think you can sell the picture?"

"Possibly. And if I do, I'll compensate you. Standard rate for models. It's right there in the release." She pointed to a paragraph in the middle of the first page.

"You don't have to pay me." His tone took on a slight defensive edge.

"It's customary. I won't take no for an answer. Besides, I haven't sold the photo yet and may not. But just in case—" she flipped the top sheet over "—you sign at the bottom of page two."

Conner hesitated and glanced at his friend. "Would you?"

"Hell yes," Gavin said. "Be a kick to see my ugly mug on a calendar."

"On one condition." Conner returned the signed release form to Dallas. "I'd like a copy of the picture. Two. One for me, one for my mom."

"Deal. I'll bring you a whole dozen tomorrow. Different sizes."

"No need to make a special trip."

"I don't mind. I have to take a few more pictures of the sanctuary. If you have the time for me, that is."

"He'll make the time," Gavin insisted. "I want this book ready for our spring donation drive."

Sage appeared in the entryway between the kitchen and hall, Milo in her arms. "You done here, Dallas? I have a sleepy young man who's ready for bed."

Gavin raised his arms over his head in a huge stretch. "He's not the only one."

"I should get going." Conner pushed away from the table. "From the way things are shaping up, I have a long day ahead of me tomorrow."

"See you later." Dallas hoped her eagerness didn't sound in her voice.

It obviously did, for Sage stared openly. Gavin, too.

Conner's look—filled with longing—was the one that really got to her.

A SMALL NIGHT-LIGHT LIT the corner of the nursery with the rocking chair. Dallas settled onto the chair, a fed and cooing Milo in her lap. Sage perched on a footstool painted with Mother Goose characters, and watched her son, an expression of devotion on her face.

"Are you sure it's bedtime, Mom?" Dallas arched her brows. "He's acting wide-awake to me."

"He'll get sleepy once you start rocking him. The kid has zero staying power."

Dallas adjusted Milo, nestling his head in the crook of her elbow and his bottom on her tummy. Pushing with the ball of one foot, she set the chair in motion. He gazed up at her with curious gray-blue eyes, shoved a pudgy fist into his mouth and gurgled happily.

She fell instantly in love. "If you ever need a babysitter, I'm available."

"You're going to have to fight Wayne for that privilege."

Dallas thought of Sage's father-in-law and nodded confidently. "I can take him. I will, too, for a chance to spend time with this handsome guy." She leaned down and bumped foreheads with Milo.

"I'll keep you in mind for a backup."

Without thinking, Dallas began humming a lullaby. "Hush Little Baby." The one her mother used to sing to her and Liam.

Cassie stuck her head in the door, Blue by her side, and announced in a loud whisper, "We're done with our homework. Dad supervised, and he guarantees Isa's going to ace her spelling test. Can we watch TV now?"

Sage smiled fondly at Cassie. "Sure thing, *mija*. But only until nine."

Dallas knew enough Spanish to understand the fond endearment. How sweet. Sage and Cassie's affection appeared genuine and—this was the important part—natural. Dallas thought of her own family.

Hank cared for her; she knew that in her heart. But they definitely lacked the easy camaraderie Sage and Cassie shared. At this stage, Dallas and Hank were unlikely to find it. Unless, possibly, one of them tried harder.

If she tried harder.

"You handle it well," Dallas told Sage.

"Handle what?"

"Cassie. Your relationship with her. Can't always be easy, raising someone else's child."

"Oh, trust me, it's not. She's capable of being a thirteen-year-old hot mess when she wants. There are days I want to… Well, I can't say. You might change your opinion of me."

"Impossible."

"Both Gavin and I are learning our way with Cassie."

"From what I can see, he's doing okay, too."

"Once they connected, and that did take a while, it was as if she'd never grown up anywhere else but at Powell Ranch and with him."

"It still amazes me that he saw her only a few times before she moved to Arizona."

"Her mother calls every few days, but we don't talk about her much as a family. Or Isa's father, for that matter. He sees her once a month. Not at first, mind you. Last summer he had a change of heart. His new wife's influence, if you ask me. I, however, wouldn't care if he dropped off the face of the earth. Not after what he did to me. But for Isa's sake, I allow the visits and keep my mouth shut. She hasn't quite fit in with her other siblings or stepmother yet, though they're making progress."

"It might never get any better, take it from me."

"Why do you say that?" Sage leaned forward to study Milo, who'd begun to drift off.

"My mom's been married to Hank for twenty-four years. I still don't feel like we're a family or have anything remotely close to what you and Cassie have."

"Is he that bad?"

"No. He was strict with me and Liam when we were kids. I get that now. Rules were his way of showing he cared."

"Most kids struggle with structure. Cassie certainly does. Isa, too."

"Yeah, but Gavin's easygoing. Hank's as straight-laced as they come. Prefers a traditional home. Man is the provider, woman cares for the man and the children. Gavin's not like that."

"Dealing with your spouse's children requires walking a very narrow line." Sage stood and lifted Milo from Dallas's arms. "Not everyone manages that successfully." She carried the sleeping baby to the crib, laid him down and adjusted the blanket.

Dallas remained in the rocking chair, her arms achingly empty. Before too long, she reminded herself, she'd be holding her own son or daughter. Except on the days Richard had the baby. How would she cope for even an hour without her precious child?

That was the one and only reason she could think of to accept Richard's marriage proposal.

Dallas pushed up from the rocking chair and tiptoed behind Sage out of the nursery and into the hall. There, she paused.

Right now, at this moment, she was strong. A few months from now, or after the baby was born, she might turn into an emotional weakling. One susceptible to marrying a man she didn't love just because she couldn't bear giving up her baby on alternate weekends.

Chapter Seven

Conner waited on the stoop in front of the barn office, watching Dallas attempt to start her car. How many times was she going to let the engine grind like that before she gave up and went in search of help? He supposed he should go over and save the battery before she drained it completely, or flooded the engine with gasoline.

She was just shoving the driver's door open when he approached. Her welcoming smile made him glad he'd stopped by the office to have a look at tomorrow's schedule before heading to the apartment.

"Doesn't sound like you're going anywhere soon."

"Whatever was wrong with the car last night is worse now." She expelled a frustrated breath. "My fault. I should've taken it in this morning to be looked at, but I was running late."

Conner didn't think he would ever understand female logic, though it did intrigue him. "Pop the hood. Let's see what's wrong." He removed the penlight he usually carried from his pocket. "My guess is your starter's faulty," he said, after a brief inspection.

"Are you sure it's not the battery?"

"You doubt me?" He found the prospect more amusing than insulting.

"No. I'm simply hoping for an easier fix. One that could be accomplished with a pair of jumper cables."

"We can always try that. If it would make you happy."

She wrinkled her brow. "How sure are you it's the starter?"

"More sure it's the starter than the battery or your alternator."

"Great." She glanced around.

He could almost hear her mentally exploring her options.

"I'll drive you home. You can call your mechanic tomorrow and have the car picked up. Or Gavin and I can figure out a way to tow it there."

"I can't impose on you like that. Let me call my parents."

"It's no imposition."

"I live off of Hayden and Indian Bend Road. Twenty-five miles away. That's far."

"You could spend the night here." He gave her a slow smile. "No!"

Her alarm at his suggestion was almost as amusing as her mistrust in his mechanic skills. "You sure? Because the sofa bed in Gavin's family room is pretty comfortable. I've slept there once or twice myself."

"The sofa bed?"

His smile grew. "Where'd you think I meant?"

"Nowhere. Gavin's." She fussed with her hair. "You were joking, weren't you?"

"You're an easy mark." He couldn't see her face, but he'd guess her cheeks were bright red and probably quite appealing.

Just as well it was dark outside. Conner already found her appealing enough as it was, and harder every day to resist.

"Come on." He nodded at her front seat. "Grab your purse and anything else you need and lock up your car."

"Thank you." She collected her belongings and shut the door. "Seems I'm doing that a lot lately."

"Having car trouble?"

"Thanking you," she said, as they began walking toward the apartment and Conner's truck.

"I don't mind helping you, Dallas." He opened his truck door, supported her elbow as she placed a foot on the side rail and hopped in. "That's what friends do for each other."

Friends, he reminded himself again as her shapely backside plunked down onto the seat. He had no business dating any woman, much less a pregnant one whose baby daddy was determined to marry her.

On the way to her place, she told him all about rocking Milo to sleep. "He's precious. Sage and Gavin are so lucky."

"In more ways than one," Conner agreed.

"Do you want kids?"

He sent her a brief look before returning his attention to the oncoming traffic.

"I shouldn't have asked that," she blurted. "It's just, you were so good with Milo at the dinner table. And you dote on your sisters."

"I do want kids. Eventually. When the timing's right."

"I used to think that, too. That I needed to have everything in order first. Husband. Job. Home. Money in the bank. Only then could I start a family. Well, as we both know, it didn't happen quite that way. And it's okay. I'm going to be fine. The baby, too."

"Because of Richard."

"Not just him."

"Has he asked you again to marry him?"

"We talk regularly," she answered tightly.

Conner took that as a yes.

He thought of his former girlfriend and her daughter. If he and Leeza had married, as he'd hinted often enough, he'd have a wife and stepdaughter to worry about in addition to himself. They wouldn't like living in an apartment on a ranch.

Leeza wouldn't, he corrected himself. Her daughter was another story.

"Have you ever considered leaving the corporate world for

good?" Dallas bit her lip. "There I go again, asking personal questions that are none of my business."

"No, never. I refuse to quit looking for a job. I made a mistake, taking a few months off after my termination. I assumed, with my qualifications, I'd find employment right away."

"A mistake? Why? Don't you enjoy working with horses?"

"It's not enough."

"You miss the money."

He turned off the 101 Freeway at the Indian Bend exit. "I'd be a liar if I said I didn't enjoy the luxuries my old salary afforded me. And saying I miss the challenges of redesigning and updating antiquated production systems is only half-true."

"Pride?"

"In part. I was raised by a dad who taught me a man's worth is measured by certain things. Among them, his ability to provide for his family. I'm not in that position anymore. But I will be again. Soon," he added with determination.

"You do know the ability to provide isn't important to some women." Dallas looked out the window rather than at him.

"Would you respect a man who earned substantially less money than you?"

"I respect a man who works hard, regardless of what he earns."

"But would you consider marrying him?"

"That's not a fair question."

"Sure it is."

She turned away from the window to stare pointedly at him. "If I loved someone, his earning ability wouldn't matter."

"Hmmm."

"You don't believe me?"

"A man worth his salt wouldn't marry without having a good job, love or not."

She pondered his remark for a moment. "Would you go out on a date with me if you hadn't lost your job?"

In a heartbeat. He'd have been calling her the second he learned she and Richard were through, baby on the way or not.

"What's the difference, since I did lose my job?"

"I want to know."

"Remind me, is your street east or west of Hayden?"

He felt her gaze on him, searching his profile for the answer he'd refused to give.

"East," she said after a long pause.

Their conversation came to a halt, except for Dallas giving Conner directions to her town house.

He pulled up to the curb on the quiet side street and shut off the truck.

"You don't have to walk me to my door," she insisted.

"Yes, I do."

"Another one of those *certain things* your dad taught you about men?"

"Can't help it."

He hurried, but didn't quite reach the passenger door before she was out and on the sidewalk. She rummaged in her purse for her keys. Finding them at last, she started up the lit walkway toward her door, Conner beside her.

"I'd invite you in but, given our recent conversation, I'm assuming you'd refuse."

She looked every bit as appealing in the city moonlight as she had in the country.

"You can't possibly know how much I wish circumstances were different."

"I think I do know." She lifted her face to his. "Because I wish they were different, too."

His heart jumped. If not for the minuscule thread of control he still maintained, he'd wrap his arms around her waist and find out at long last how she felt pressed flush against him.

"Dallas."

"Yes?" She bit her bottom lip, drew it between her teeth.

He swallowed and wondered at what point his throat had gone bone-dry. "You have to stop doing that."

"Why?" Without looking away from him, she dropped her purse and portfolio onto the ground.

Oh, hell.

There were a hundred, a thousand, reasons not to get involved with her, and only one reason to: he was crazy about her.

And just plain crazy.

He had to be. If not, he wouldn't be sliding his hands into her open jacket and seeking her mouth with his.

Dallas went pliant in his arms the instant their lips touched, all lush, warm curves and intoxicating scent.

He was drowning, losing the battle, and he didn't care. Not about anything or anyone but her. He wanted more, of her, of their kiss.

Stumbling, he turned them both and pressed her into the front door. Then groaned when she curled her arms about his neck and tugged his head down, rising on tiptoes to meet him.

All thoughts of resistance fled as his hands moved from her waist to her hips, liking the firm yet subtle slope of her womanly shape. Her own hands were also busy. They traveled the length of his back, gripping him with a need more ardent than Conner's, if that was possible.

The kiss was nothing and everything like he'd remembered from that one evening years ago.

She made a soft, sexy sound of pleasure and arched into him. It was enough to remind Conner of their surroundings.

Rational thought seeped slowly in, urging him to stop before they went too far. Nothing could ever come from this one moment of insanity. He couldn't take care of her the way she needed to be taken care of. The way Richard could. Would.

Conner pulled back, the blood rushing through his veins causing a deafening roar in his ears.

No, wait. The roaring was a car. It tore down the street, growing louder, and coming to a gravel-crunching stop behind Conner's truck.

Dallas and Conner flew apart, and not a second too soon.

The car door opened and Richard emerged. He took one look at the two of them standing on her front porch step, and stopped cold in his tracks.

"CONNER." RICHARD ADVANCED, hand outstretched. "I didn't expect to find you here."

That made two of them.

"How've you been?" Conner accepted the other man's gesture of goodwill, glad Dallas hadn't turned on the exterior light. Richard wouldn't notice the line of sweat beading his brow.

He could feel Dallas's eyes on him. She looked frazzled. Embarrassed. Guilty.

If Richard hadn't suspected anything before, he did now.

Conner kept his cool, his grip firm.

"I've been all right," Richard said evenly.

He was dressed as always when not at the office. Jeans, athletic shoes and a hoodie with the company logo on the front.

They'd been an unlikely pair, the jock and the cowboy. And yet they'd been buddies. Good ones. Their love of their work and dedication to Triad bonding them.

For the first time since he'd been let go, Conner missed their friendship.

"He brought me home," Dallas explained, her breathlessness a giveaway. "My car wouldn't start. I'm having it towed in the morning."

"You were at Powell Ranch?"

"I delivered some pictures. For the book."

"That's right. The book." Richard visibly relaxed. "Nice of you to bring her home."

He and Dallas weren't engaged anymore. Conner had nothing to feel guilty about. Yet he did. This was the father of her baby. The man who wanted to make her his wife.

"Not a problem." Conner took a step back. "I should get going."

"No, stay!" Dallas's outburst appeared to take the three of them by surprise. "What are you doing here, Richard?" she asked nervously.

"I've been trying to reach you all afternoon and evening. I have some health insurance papers for you to sign. When you didn't answer your phone, I got worried. Thought something must be wrong."

"Oh, that's right." Dallas rummaged in her purse for her cell phone. "I switched the ringer to silent and forgot to turn it back on."

"Don't you check your phone?"

"I was busy," she quipped defensively.

When Richard's gaze landed on Conner again, it was direct and unwavering. "Yeah, I see that."

"Sorry about my phone," Dallas said, "but as you can clearly tell, I'm fine. And tired."

Richard ignored the undisguised hint to leave. "I won't keep you long, I promise."

It really was past time for Conner to go. Kisses aside, he had no claim on Dallas. "I'll see you tomorrow," he said to her, imagining how their goodbye might have differed without Richard's surprise appearance.

"What's going on tomorrow?" Richard asked, suddenly all ears.

"I'm taking pictures of Prince. The mustang stallion," she clarified, at his confused expression.

"That's right. For the book again."

Conner didn't understand Richard's cavalier dismissal. The book was important to Dallas, and so should be to him, as well.

Not Conner's problem. Touching his fingers to the brim of his cowboy hat, he walked away.

"Conner." Richard caught up with him at the end of Dallas's walkway. "Since you're here, there's something I want to ask you."

He must have seen more than Conner originally suspected.

There would be no explaining or defending himself. Not to Richard.

"What's up?"

"I don't have the right to ask, and I sure as hell wouldn't blame you for not answering me."

A different approach than Conner would have taken. In Richard's shoes, he'd have led with a right hook.

"Just say it, Richard."

"I'm…" He chuckled humorlessly. "I'm having trouble with some of your former team members. Most of them, actually. Rosco Burnes and Evelyn Lancaster in particular. I understood at first. They liked you and were unhappy to see you leave. I figured I'd give them a couple months to adjust. Only they haven't. I can handle their insubordination. It's the stirring up trouble I don't like. Aligning the others against me."

Richard wanted help managing employees? Conner thought he must have misheard. Richard, the great department head. The one with more experience, according to the HR rep who'd issued Conner his pink slip. The one who used to brag about his production record and fat profit margin. He was seeking Conner's advice?

"Rosco is bullheaded and Evelyn's officious." That was all Richard was going to get from him.

The man's next words changed his mind.

"I'd hate for them to lose their jobs."

"Are you going to fire them?" Conner's hackles rose.

"They've had three warnings each. Two verbal and one written. You know company policy."

He did. Rosco and Evelyn had reached their warning limits. A fourth one would result in probation. Then, leave without pay. After that, termination.

As much as Conner appreciated their loyalty, as much as he secretly cheered Rosco and Evelyn for giving Richard grief, he didn't want them to lose their jobs. Not on his account.

"Ask Evelyn about her grandchildren," he said.

"What?"

"She has pictures of them in her cubicle, right?"

Richard shrugged. "I haven't paid any attention."

And that was a large part of his problem. He drew a very thick, black line between work and personal life. He never crossed it and preferred no one else did, either. He also tended to micromanage new employees and those he didn't quite trust. Conner was sure all his former team members fell into the latter category.

"Evelyn is a proud grandmother. There's nothing she'd rather talk about. Mention you're going to be a father soon. She'll melt."

"I don't like discussing Dallas's pregnancy at work."

"Make an exception. You don't have to go into details. And assign Rosco the weekly scheduling."

"I've always done the scheduling."

"Give him the job for a month. If he doesn't meet your standards, offer him some guidelines. He'll get it right. And you'll free yourself of one task."

"I'm not sure he's capable of it."

"He'll surprise you. He did me." Conner took a step toward his truck. "Once Rosco and Evelyn are on board, the rest of the department will follow."

"I'm not a touchy-feely manager."

"You don't have to be. A little bit of sincere interest in your employees' lives, a few tasks delegated, will go a long way."

Richard nodded. "Okay. Thanks."

"Tell everyone I said hello."

"I'll do that."

Conner decided Richard would probably deliver the message. And perhaps, if his former team members knew that he and Richard were on speaking terms, tenuous as those terms might be, they'd be more inclined to cooperate. No more people at Triad Energy would lose their jobs if Conner could help it.

His last sight of Dallas before he drove away was her opening her front door, Richard trailing her inside, his hands shoved in his hoodie pockets. He'd said he wanted to talk about health insurance. Was that was an excuse, and his real intention to pressure her into accepting his marriage proposal?

Jealousy gnawed at Conner.

If Richard did convince Dallas to marry him, Conner wouldn't stand in the way. She'd do what was best for her and the baby. As was right.

The lights of Mustang Valley were just coming into view when his cell phone chimed. Considering the hour, he assumed it was either one of his sisters or an emergency at the ranch.

It was neither. Dallas's number flashed on the display.

Excitement, then trepidation, shot through him. He suppressed both. "Hey."

"Hope it's not too late to call."

"Is something wrong?"

Had Richard argued with her? Or was she announcing that they were back together?

"Everything's fine. I just wanted to say you're a really nice guy, Conner."

"I am?"

"You didn't have to help Richard. In fact, nobody would blame you if you'd told him where to stuff it. Especially your former employees."

Richard had talked to Dallas about their conversation. Interesting.

"I won't lie. I thought about doing a lot worse than telling him where, and how deep, to stuff it."

She laughed good-naturedly. Even over a phone line, it had the ability to lighten his mood. Warm him. Make him think of her pretty brown eyes, shining with merriment.

Conner stopped his truck at the entrance to Powell Ranch. He didn't want to concentrate on anything except the smile in her voice.

"I'm glad you didn't."

"I care about the people at Triad. It's not their fault they're saddled with Richard as a boss."

She laughed again, and promptly sobered. "You're a good person for someone to have on their side."

"I try."

"The kind of person I'd want on my side," she added softly.

It was more than he should admit, but he said it anyway. What was the worst that could happen?

"You do. And always will."

"I'm glad. Good night, Conner."

She disconnected without waiting for him to say goodnight in return.

Conner's heart didn't stop slamming into his rib cage for several long minutes, after which he put the truck in gear and continued up the long driveway to the ranch.

Chapter Eight

Dallas couldn't remember seeing Powell Ranch so busy. Granted, it was Saturday, a day when many of the residents of Mustang Village and nearby Scottsdale took riding lessons, exercised their horses and embarked on trail rides. The unseasonably mild weather was an added bonus. By next week, November would be upon them and the temperature was bound to drop.

Grabbing her camera bag from the passenger seat, she left her car and strode toward the office in the barn. It had been her intention to come out last Monday and take pictures of Prince, as she'd told Conner she would. Several unscheduled and well-paying jobs had caused her to postpone the trip.

She'd spoken with him twice since then, the second time about what day would be best for them to get together. They hadn't mentioned their kiss on her doorstep or the details of Richard's visit.

She was certain Richard had sensed the undercurrents between her and Conner. He wasn't stupid and he wasn't blind. But he hadn't asked any questions, for which she was grateful, and had left shortly after explaining about the insurance papers.

It was none of his business who she dated, anyway. They'd called off their engagement months ago. If he happened to acquire a new girlfriend, she wouldn't object.

A new girlfriend who might well be at his place during his scheduled day with their baby. A girlfriend who'd possibly feed and change her child's diapers. Rock him or her to sleep, as Dallas had Milo.

Nausea struck, and she pressed a hand to her middle.

She had to stop thinking about Richard and another woman. About her and Conner, too. They *weren't* dating and wouldn't start.

Maybe they'd date later, after the baby was, say, a year or two old.

What about Richard and his future, potential girlfriend? Would she and not Dallas watch her child take his or her first step? Speak his or her first word?

This truly had to end. Right now. If not, she'd make herself sick overthinking things.

It was probably just as well she'd been busy this past week. The separation from Conner had grounded her. Given her time to clear her head and put their temporary foray into madness into perspective. It was simply a kiss. The spontaneous product of attraction and impulse. An isolated occurrence.

As she climbed the three steps to the office, her heart rate increased. Her palms, she noticed, were damp, and her entire body hummed with a pleasant anticipation.

So much for being grounded and acquiring perspective.

Tugging on the hem of her sweater, she pasted a friendly, but not too friendly, smile on her face and swung open the office door.

Conner wasn't there, as per their prearranged plan. Instead, Gavin sat at the desk, staring at a computer monitor. Dallas read the flashing banner advertising equine medical supplies.

He glanced up as she entered. "Hey, girl. How's it going?"

"Good." She wavered between relief and disappointment.

"Conner's on his way back from the rodeo arena."

"Oh, okay."

He was coming. He hadn't stood her up. The relief she felt now was of an entirely different nature.

"Can I get you a coffee?" Gavin nodded at the pot warming on the file cabinet.

"No, thanks." She studied the office. It was functional and hardly fancy, the furniture old but sturdy. "I can wait outside if you're busy."

"I'll go with you." He stood, closed the webpage and reached for the cowboy hat resting on the corner of his desk. "Any excuse to get out of ordering supplies online. Whatever happened to catalogs and 800 numbers?"

"There's a ton of people here today," Dallas commented as they stepped outside.

"Thanks to you."

"Me?"

"Those photographs you sent to the local media." He zipped up his Carhartt vest. "Apparently they're generating a buzz. Did you see the news Wednesday evening?"

"I missed it. I was photographing the Carefree Fine Arts Festival."

"The station ran a segment. Mentioned the ranch by name. We've been flooded with calls since. Most people want to know if we found the mare and colt. Quite a few were interested in our services." He nodded at the dozen horses and riders gathering in front of the main arena. "We have a record number of trail rides scheduled for today. I had to recruit a few of Ethan's rodeo buddies to help out."

"That's great, Gavin." She patted his arm affectionately. "I'm so glad."

The Powells were still recovering from the financial disaster that had cost them their cattle operation after Gavin's mother died, several years ago. If the mare and colt weren't ever found, at least something good had come from her photographs.

"Sage found the news clip on YouTube," Gavin said. "She's better with computers than me. I'll have her send you the link. We're going to add it to the ranch and sanctuary websites."

"Any sightings of the mare and colt?"

"Not a one, unfortunately."

"You've been searching for them, though."

"When we can. Conner and Clay went out Monday and again on Thursday. No luck. I spoke to the Forest Service. They told me if we do find the horses, they'll let us keep them as long as no one comes forward with proof of ownership."

"That much is good at least."

"We're thinking of trying the same trick we used to capture Prince."

"A Judas horse. I remember." Dallas had learned all about it while working with the writer for the book.

"Yeah." Gavin nodded. "The mare was raised with other horses, that's obvious. If Ethan and I hadn't come barreling up that hill on our ATVs, Conner would have had her tied and ready to be led home."

Dallas remembered her frustration when the mare took off at the sudden noise.

"We're thinking of erecting a similar makeshift pen in the box canyon," Gavin continued. "Put a couple horses in there for a day or two and spread out some hay. With luck, she'll come out of hiding."

"She and the colt have to be hungry."

Gavin's cell rang before he could respond. "Yeah, Conner." He paused and looked at Dallas. "She's here now. I'll tell her." Gavin disconnected. "He's on his way. Be another fifteen minutes."

"Is Sage around? I could visit the baby."

"She's with Sierra. They took the kids on a play date." Gavin looked bemused. "As if my two-year-old nephew is interested in his three-month-old cousin."

"Not yet. But one day those two boys will be close as brothers and getting into the same kind of trouble you and Ethan did."

"God help us all."

"Gavin!" A man holding a handsome Thoroughbred hollered and waved him over. "Got a second to look at this fella's limp?"

"Be right back," Gavin told Dallas.

"No rush. I'll just wander."

She didn't get too far before Gavin's stepdaughter plodded up on a swaybacked gelding.

"Hello, Mizz Sorz-son," she said, butchering Dallas's last name.

"Hello to you, too, Miss Isa. And don't you think you should call me Dallas? We've been friends awhile."

"Gavin says I'm supposed to be polite."

Dallas went over and stroked the horse's velvety nose. "You have my permission to call me that."

"Really?" The girl grinned, leaned down and wrapped her arms around the horse's neck. "But I might have to call you Mizz Sorz-son in front of Gavin."

"Is he strict with you and Cassie?" Dallas wondered if his parenting style was more like Hank's than she'd initially thought. If strictness was typical of all stepfathers.

"Kinda." Isa straightened, her mouth scrunched to one side as she pondered Dallas's question. "Not like my mom. Cassie and I have sooo many chores." She expelled a tired breath, as if the burden placed on her was unbearable. "Gavin just wants us to use manners with anyone who comes to the ranch. Always say Mister and Mizz because we rep-per-sent the Powells."

Dallas had to laugh. Isa's impersonation of Gavin was spot on. "You're doing a fine job."

"Why ya here? You taking more pictures?"

"Of Prince. I'm waiting on your uncle Conner."

"You wannna ride Chico?" She patted the horse's neck.

The old gelding had been standing patiently, head hanging and eyes drifting close. He completely ignored his young rider, who constantly wiggled and jiggled and fidgeted, standing up in the stirrups, only to plop back down.

Dallas was convinced a giant crack in the earth could open up in front of the horse and he'd sleep through it.

She did miss riding. Her doctor had advised she could continue with her normal activities at this stage of her pregnancy as long as she was careful. What better horse to ride than one entrusted with an unsupervised seven-year-old?

"Only if you watch me," Dallas said. "And we ride in the round pen."

"Yay! You hear that, Chico?"

Dallas walked alongside Isa and Chico to the pen, which had been recently vacated by the man with the limping Thoroughbred. Slinging her camera bag over a fence post, she watched as Isa hopped from the saddle and, holding on to the horn, dropped the last two feet to the ground. Chico didn't move, reassuring Dallas that riding him would be completely safe.

"Here." Isa tossed Dallas the reins and scrambled up the fence, where she perched on the top rung.

Dallas mounted Chico, who remained completely disinterested in the change of riders. She nudged him into a walk, her hands relaxed as she guided him in a circle. Not that the old horse needed much guiding. He knew his job.

The sun on her face, the breeze tickling her hair, the sound of Chico's hooves tromping through the soft dirt, the McDowell Mountains standing tall and proud to the south—it was an absolutely perfect experience.

"Make him trot," Isa called out. "He'll do it. He's just lazy."

"Lazy is the right speed. Besides, I'm not sure trotting would be good for me."

"Why?" Isa wrinkled her small brow in puzzlement.

"Because I'm having a baby."

"You are?" The girl's mouth fell open. "Seriously?"

"Didn't your parents tell you?"

She shook her head, and then announced proudly, "I know all about having babies. Where they come from. How they're born." She rubbed her belly. "Mama told me they grow in here. In the u-tar-us."

"They do." Dallas would rather avoid any discussion of human reproduction with Isa, and changed the subject. "How old is Chico?"

The girl was not to be deterred. "When Mama had Milo, she let me go to the doctor with her and see pictures of him on this machine. His heart was beating, like, a million miles an hour, and I could see his arm moving." Awe shone on her face and altered the quality of her voice. "Did you do that? See your baby on a machine?"

"Not yet. Probably next month." How to introduce a different topic? Dallas racked her brain as Chico continued trudging in circles.

"Can I go with you when you do?" Isa asked.

"Um…" Dallas hadn't even decided if she was going to bring Richard. She supposed she should ask him. "Let me talk to your mother about it first." A cop-out, but she didn't know how else to fend off Isa's request. "Where's your sister today?"

It turned out that Dallas didn't need another distraction attempt. Conner's truck rambled past, on the way to his apartment, she assumed. Except the truck came to a sudden, gravel-crunching stop.

Conner jumped out and ran toward them.

"Hi, Uncle Conner."

He ignored Isa, jerked open the gate and stormed into the pen, waving his arms in front of Chico. "Whoa, boy."

Chico obediently stopped, as if that was his intention all along, and gawked at the human suddenly blocking his path.

So did Dallas. "What's wrong?"

He took hold of Chico's bridle. "Get down now."

"Why?"

"You agreed, no riding."

"Into the mountains. This is Chico. We both know he isn't going to do anything."

"Dallas, please," he pleaded. "Even a small risk isn't worth it."

The concern in his voice swayed her when she would have put up a fight. He cared.

"All right." She gripped the saddle horn as Isa had done and swung her right leg over Chico's behind.

Reaching the ground, she spun, only to find herself in Conner's arms. Then in his embrace.

CONNER HELD ON TO DALLAS, relieved she was safe from harm. It wasn't his intention to put them in yet another compromising position, but she'd given him a start. Yes, old Chico was a dependable mount, but he was an animal, and therefore unpredictable. If she by chance fell...

"I'm okay," Dallas muttered into his jacket front.

Realizing his grip was tighter than necessary, he released her, only to study her from head to toe. "You sure?"

"I'm sure." She smiled.

He couldn't kiss her. Not with Isa and half of Mustang Village watching. And they were watching. Conner slamming on his truck brakes had guaranteed that.

But he wanted to kiss her. Badly.

He would again, he vowed. When he landed a decent job. Secured his house from the clutches of the bank. Purchased a new vehicle suitable for transporting a mother and child. Wasn't mooching off his friends.

"Believe me," she said. "I wouldn't have ridden Chico if I thought it was risky."

"I know. But do me a favor. Don't ride him or any horse until after the baby's born. My nerves can't take it."

"All right, I won't. I promise. Not where you can see me, anyway."

"Dallas!" His fingers found her shoulders and squeezed.

She laughed. That incredible, intoxicating laugh of hers. "You're very gullible. Has anyone ever told you that?"

"My mother lost two babies. Miscarriages. The first from stepping off a curb and falling down. It's one of the reasons her marriage to my dad hit the skids."

Dallas instantly sobered. "I didn't know."

"I just wouldn't want to see you—or anyone—suffer."

"Thanks." She reached up and cupped his cheek, let her thumb skim the line of his jaw. "You're one of the good ones, Conner."

He tensed, a fiery current zinging through him.

"Hey, Uncle Conner!" Isa jumped down from the fence, landing feetfirst in the soft dirt with a thud. "Are you and Dallas, I mean Mizz Sorz-son, boyfriend and girlfriend?"

"We're just friends." He handed Isa the reins, then tugged on the brim of her crooked ball cap. "No boy and girl in front of it." To emphasize the point, he stepped away from Dallas.

"Hmm." Isa scrutinized them, her mouth pursed. "It sorta looks like you are."

"Enough from you, pip-squeak."

More to shut her up than anything else, Conner grabbed her around the middle and tickled her ribs. She giggled and tried to squirm away. When she nearly succeeded, he lifted her up and plunked her into the saddle.

"Now, go find your dad," he told her.

She bent down and gave his neck a hug. "I love you, Uncle Conner."

His chest tightened. She'd never said anything like that before. "Right back at you, pip-squeak."

He shot a quick, embarrassed glance at Dallas. She was staring at him as if he had discovered the cure to end world hunger.

Women. They were an enigma. One impossible to solve.

"See ya later, Mizz Sorz-son." Isa nudged Chico into a walk.

"Call me Dallas," she hollered after the girl.

"You two pals now?" Conner asked.

"Not like you two."

"I was just being nice to her."

"Right. It's not as if you really love Isa."

He didn't answer.

Dallas grinned and grabbed her camera bag.

Conner had his hand on the gate, ready to close it, when a rider approached. "You want to use the pen?"

"If you're done," the woman answered pleasantly. She sat astride a sleek ebony horse that pranced eagerly in place.

"That's one of the rehabilitated wild mustangs from the sanctuary," he informed Dallas.

She stopped and turned back. "Do you think she'd mind if I took her picture?"

"Ask her while I park my truck."

Dallas was bursting with excitement when they met up five minutes later. "I got some great shots. That woman truly adores her horse. Did you train him?"

"Me? No. He's one of Ethan's success stories. When that horse was first brought in from the reservation after a roundup, he was considered incorrigible."

"Well, not anymore."

"Ethan's the best trainer in these parts."

"You're pretty good yourself."

Conner shrugged off the compliment. "I've only been working with the wild mustangs the last three months."

"How's the job search going? Did Hank line you up with any good prospects?"

Dallas was being nice, expressing an interest. But dammit, Conner wished she'd quit bringing up his lack of employment every time they were together.

"He did put me in contact with one company. A paper product manufacturer in Chandler."

"And?"

"The vice president interviewed me."

"And?" she prompted when he hesitated.

"It was a courtesy to Hank. They'd more or less filled the position already. With a woman. Seems the company has a policy regarding the ratio of male and female supervisors. To avoid any accusations of discrimination."

"That's rough. Denied a job because you're a guy."

"I've been turned down for worse reasons."

"Any other leads? It didn't occur to me to ask, but Hank might also know a reputable headhunter."

Three leads this week and they'd all gone nowhere. Conner would rather stick pins in his eyes than tell Dallas about them.

"Today's kind of a celebration," he said as they neared the horse barn. "Prince is being bred to his hundredth mare since the Powells have owned him."

His tactic worked. She was sidetracked.

"I'd love pictures of that. Would Gavin mind?"

"Watching a pair of breeding horses isn't for the faint of heart."

"I can handle it. I know all about the birds and the bees." She patted her stomach. "Obviously."

"Horses kick and bite. You could get hurt."

"I'll be careful."

"It may not matter. Prince will have one thing on his mind and no regard for manners."

"That's why zoom lenses were invented." She stopped abruptly and drew in a breath. "He's beautiful. I've seen him before, but not like this."

They were in sight of Prince's quarters, a specially designed stall at the end of the row. He stood at the railing, watching a small herd graze in the nearby pasture, his head held high and tail arched.

Several times a week Gavin put Prince in the pasture with one or two nonaggressive geldings. Like most studs, Prince could be difficult to handle, especially when there were mares in heat. Running and socializing with other horses helped to calm him.

Contact with people did, as well. He liked Gavin best and was reasonably fond of Ethan, who'd broken Prince to ride last winter. Conner he tolerated.

As they neared the stall, Prince went from standing to prancing back and forth, proudly showing off his form. He stopped just as suddenly and whinnied shrilly, his attention on the mare motel next door.

"I swear, that horse has a sixth sense. He always knows when it's breeding day."

Dallas reached into her bag and removed her camera. Dipping and moving from side to side, she snapped away. "How close can I get?"

"You're close enough." Conner held her in place by clutching her sweater sleeve.

"The bars of the stall are in the way." She lowered the camera. "Any chance you can put Prince in the pasture? I'd love some pictures of him at a full gallop. That mane and tail of his are amazing."

"Maybe. After the breeding. If he's settled down enough."

"Can I pet him? Will he mind?"

Conner marveled at how her mind jumped from one subject to the next at the speed of light. "Let me go first. He's made a lot of progress, but he's not completely trustworthy with strangers."

Nearing the stall, Conner held his hand out in front of him. "Easy does it. That's right."

Prince rushed over to the railing, blowing lustily.

Conner stroked his face, his movements slow and steady. "Good boy."

The horse dropped his head, indicating he wanted a scratching between the ears.

"He doesn't look so tough." Dallas inched closer, not waiting for Conner's okay.

"He's like any guy. There's always one thing that turns him from a lion into a kitten."

"Is that so?"

"See for yourself."

Prince had begun to relax, his ear lying back rather than standing straight up. Another minute and he'd be rolling on the ground, hooves in the air, begging for a tummy rub.

Dallas placed a tentative hand on the side of Prince's sleek black neck. "What's the one thing that turns you into a kitten?"

She had to ask? The answer was standing right beside him, her elbow brushing his.

"A neck rub," he answered, choosing a safer answer.

"Seems you and Prince are a lot alike."

"Apparently."

Her eyes lit with mischief. "I'll have to remember that. If I ever want to wheedle a favor from you."

He nearly groaned out loud, imagining her hands on him, kneading his flesh.

"We should find Gavin. If you want those pictures of Prince."

They located him in the arena, instructing a class of beginner riders. The youngsters zigzagged their mounts around a series of poles, practicing their reining skills.

"Maybe we should come back later," Dallas suggested.

"Give him a minute."

"If you've got something to do, somewhere to be—"

"You're my job for the next hour."

"And then?" she asked.

"I'm due at the rodeo arena. Clay's expecting a crowd tonight."

"Bull riding?"

"Tie-down roping and team roping."

"You ever miss competing?"

"Not one bit."

"It's exciting."

"I prefer getting my thrills other ways than being launched from the back of a bucking bull."

"Like?"

There she went again, asking questions, when the answer was standing within touching distance.

And here he was again, supplying a safe answer. "Training wild mustangs."

Gavin sauntered over to the arena fence, and none too soon.

Dallas made her requests. His answer to both was yes. He also cautioned her regarding the dangers of standing too close to Prince.

"If you want to bring the mare from her stall to the breeding shed," he told Conner, "I'll meet you there with Prince. She's the little chestnut beauty in number eight."

Conner didn't normally assist with the breeding. Today was evidently an exception for Dallas's benefit.

"Can I come with you?" she asked.

"Wouldn't you rather go with Gavin, since he's bringing Prince?"

"I have a question for you."

Not another one!

They started walking, and Conner mentally braced himself.

"There's a charity dinner and dance I have to attend. Two weeks from today. At the Phoenician Resort. It's sponsored by the Arizona Animal Welfare Association. They provide funding to several of the no-kill animal shelters where I volunteer. The event raises a lot of money."

"You the official photographer?"

They entered the mare motel with its enclosed stalls, most of them occupied.

"Actually, I'm attending. As a guest. I've done two small shoots for the AAWA and would like to do more. This is an opportunity for me to finagle some face time with the directors."

"What's your question?" He assumed she wanted him to give these directors a tour of the mustang sanctuary.

"Do you by chance own a suit?"

"A suit?" He'd have to wear one for the tour? "Several."

"Good. Because I'm supposed to bring an escort to the dinner."

"You're inviting me on a date?" Conner missed a step and quickly regained his balance.

"Not a date. I'm asking a *friend* to accompany me to a dinner. A business dinner. Consider it a favor." She turned wide, hopeful eyes on him. "I'll repay you with a neck rub."

A neck rub! He could barely keep his hands off her as it was. Look what had happened in the round pen earlier. Seeing her in a slinky cocktail dress would be torture.

The refusal he intended to give lodged in his throat and stayed there. When he was finally able to speak, he asked, "What time should I pick you up?"

Chapter Nine

Dallas contemplated the five dresses laid out on her mother's bed.

"What do you think?" Marina asked, fingering the closest one, a bright hibiscus print with a ruffled hem. "I've always been partial to pink on you."

"It is pretty."

And not at all Dallas's style. In her mind, huge pink flowers and ruffles didn't shout prestigious charity event. The voluminous, floor-length skirt and spaghetti straps also made her think sundress. She was attempting to disguise her growing tummy, not dress for a stroll in the park.

"But maybe a little too casual."

"Really? I wore it to Hank's company's holiday party last year."

Her mother would, and pay no heed to the stares.

Dallas wanted to attract the attention of the AAWA directors in a good way, not have them gawk at her. If all went as she hoped, they would authorize her for more shoots. She lived by what she'd preached to Conner: it wasn't what you knew but who you knew.

"This one's nice." She lifted a pale gold cocktail dress with a considerably more demure neckline.

"It seems a little underwhelming." Marina frowned slightly.

And precisely what Dallas was looking for. "But with the right jewelry and shoes, I can fancy it up."

She'd come to her mother's house in the hopes of finding a suitable dress from Marina's easy-breezy wardrobe. At nearly three months pregnant, Dallas had entered the stage where her own clothes were too snug, but she wasn't quite ready for maternity outfits. Neither was she about to purchase a dress she'd likely wear once or twice.

"I'm going to try it on." She slipped into the adjoining master bathroom and changed.

"I take it back," Marina exclaimed when Dallas emerged a few minutes later. "The dress is you."

Dallas preened in front of the mirrored closet door, agreeing with her mother. The tight, high-waisted bodice and loose skirt camouflaged her tummy while still giving her an hourglass silhouette.

"I have just the necklace." Marina went to her dresser.

Dallas waited for her to return with some gaudy, oversize bangles. Instead, she was handed a dainty emerald pendant and delicate gold chain.

"Where did you get this?" She turned the pendant over in her palm, admiring the glittering stones.

"Your father."

"I've never seen you wear it." Or had any idea that Marina owned such a treasure.

"I didn't want to upset Hank by flaunting jewelry my ex-husband bought me."

"It's exquisite." Dallas fastened the chain around her neck.

"Oh, my," Marina exclaimed softly, staring at Dallas's reflection.

"Mom, I don't care if Hank gets mad." Dallas touched the pendant, hanging just below her collarbone. "You should wear this."

"You wear it. And keep it. I always meant to give you the necklace one day. It's much more your style than mine."

"Thank you." Dallas hugged her mother tightly. She had nothing of her father's, hadn't seen or talked to him in years. The necklace would stir the few fond memories she had of him.

"You're welcome, sweetheart."

She turned back to the mirror and touched the pendant again. "Dad had his faults. Bad taste in jewelry wasn't one of them."

"He tried. One of his mistakes was thinking tokens of affection could take the place of real affection. That's what I love about Hank."

"He's affectionate?"

"Very."

Apparently only when they were alone, because Dallas couldn't ever remember seeing Hank sweep her mother into a passionate embrace or hold her hand while they walked.

Conner had done both with Dallas, and much more.

"Why did you marry Dad?" She wasn't sure she'd asked the question before.

"We were a lot alike. Both artists. I sculpted, he played guitar. We were convinced we could impact the world with our art. Sometimes I think we were too alike. Hank's solid. Dependable. He keeps me on course. That's why I thought you and Richard were such a good match."

He and Hank were definitely cut from similar cloth.

What about Conner? He seemed to Dallas a combination of both types. Solid and dependable, but with an adventurous side. Like the wild mustangs he trained.

As if reading her mind, her mother said, "Conner's one lucky man."

"Why's that?"

"He'll be with the prettiest girl at the dinner."

"It's not like… We're just friends, Mom."

"Tell me you don't find him attractive."

"I'm having a baby. He isn't going to date a pregnant woman."

"Isn't that his decision to make?"

"And mine."

"Then why did you invite him to the event, if not to start something?"

Dallas fiddled with the necklace clasp, finally securing it. "Because I need an escort. And he owns a suit."

"You like him. You always have. And he likes you."

"As friends," she repeated.

"That's a good basis for a relationship. A couple should be friends before they're lovers."

"Being lovers with Conner is the furthest thing from my mind!"

Such a bald-faced lie. What would her mother say if she found out about the kiss? *Kisses!*

She'd accuse Dallas of having feelings for Conner, and she'd be right.

Feelings that could and would go nowhere.

"Don't sell Conner short," Marina said. "He's made of stronger stuff than most men. Personally, I don't think your pregnancy will deter him."

"It *will* deter him. Every time he looks at me, he'll be reminded of Richard." Of her and Richard together.

"Hank courted me when I had two small children. He didn't think about your father when he looked at me." Marina's lips curled into a playful smile. "I made sure of it. You can do the same with Conner."

Why hadn't she been born to a more inhibited mother?

"I could, if we were interested in each other. Which we're not." If she said it enough, maybe she'd start to believe it.

"Well—" Marina unzipped the dress "—I can guarantee,

if Conner hasn't been thinking about being your lover before, he will certainly start once he sees you in this."

"Mom!"

"Just stating a fact."

Dallas took another look at herself in the mirror, recalled Conner's mouth taking possession of hers. Felt his hands mold themselves to her hips.

Yes, Conner would see her in this dress and want her.

As usual, her mother was right.

BY CONNER'S ESTIMATION, about two hours of daylight remained. If he and Javier didn't find the mare and colt by dark, they'd have to return to the ranch empty-handed. This was Conner's second venture into the mountains in the last two days. He had Dallas to thank for that.

Her photos of the injured mare appeared everywhere online, generating hundreds of thousands of hits. The story had spread across the Southwest and as far east as Oklahoma. As a result, the ranch phone had been ringing off the hook with reported sightings. Only a few were legit.

The most promising one had come from the pilot of a low-flying plane on his descent into the Scottsdale Airport. He'd supposedly spotted the mare and colt not far from Tom Thumb, a favorite picnic and rest spot for trail riders.

Yesterday, Conner and Javier, a longtime wrangler at Powell Ranch, had taken two Judas horses to the area the pilot reported. Both animals had carried pack saddles loaded with materials for a makeshift corral.

If the lure worked, as it had with Prince, the mare and colt would be waiting at the corral today, munching on hay and easy to capture. The men had brought their lariats, however, just in case.

Tom Thumb, with its distinctive rock formation, came into view. The picnic area was familiar to Conner. Last year he'd brought Leeza and her daughter here, giving them a taste of cowboy life. The little girl had loved riding and being outdoors. Her mother not so much.

"Señor Conner." Javier, who'd ridden in the lead the entire trip, pointed at a huge cholla cacti patch up ahead. "*Ten cuidado*. Be careful," he called in broken English.

"*Gracias, mi amigo.*"

There was only one drawback to bringing the wrangler: his English skills weren't the best. Which left Conner with his own thoughts for company during the ride. As was typical, his mind drifted to job hunting.

Seven more résumés sent out this week. Seven polite, form email replies stating that his résumé had been received and would be reviewed. He wasn't holding his breath. Of the seven positions, he was overqualified for four and the remaining three weren't in his field. That was how wide he'd started casting his net.

He'd made a decision while saddling up this afternoon. After the charity dinner next Saturday, he'd be seeing Dallas only for the book shoots or at Gavin's request.

No more kisses. No more finding any excuse to hold her in his arms, or call just to hear her voice on the other end of the line. No more—

"Señor Conner!" Javier exclaimed, reining his horse to a stop. "*Los caballos.*"

Excitement surged inside Conner. There, about a hundred yards ahead, were the mare and colt. They stood outside the makeshift corral, munching on hay left out the day before.

"Go slow. We don't want to scare them off." He repeated his instructions in Spanish.

Precautions were unnecessary. The starving mare and colt paid little attention to anything except the hay.

The ranch horses whinnied happily at the sight of new arrivals. Despite ample food and water, they probably hadn't liked spending the night in the mountains.

"You wait here," Conner said to the wrangler. "I'll get the mare."

On the chance that she and the colt became scared and tried to bolt, Javier would be able to block their escape.

The mare, perhaps tired, perhaps sick from infection, did nothing when Conner dismounted and approached her. The colt, though clearly agitated, remained by her side.

Conner was able to place a rope around the mare, carefully avoiding the arrows, which were still imbedded in her neck and back. Not that he'd expected differently. He motioned Javier over, gesturing that he wanted the spare halter they'd brought along.

"Easy as pie," Conner said, slipping it on the mare's head.

He took a moment to examine her. She was in about the same condition as before. Looks, however, could be deceiving. Infections like hers tended to spread deeper rather than outward, and not appear so bad on the surface.

The colt wouldn't let anyone near him, dodging Conner when he tried to pet him. They would have to trust he was fit enough to make the trip to the ranch.

"Let's get to work."

Javier nodded, and together they tethered the six adult horses to the branches of nearby trees. Confused and frightened by the strange activities, the colt trotted in circles, always within close range of his mother.

The corral, which was nothing more than orange netting strung between posts, was quickly disassembled. Conner placed the pack saddles they'd left there yesterday on the two ranch horses, and loaded the netting and posts.

Within half an hour, they were ready to start for home. More than once Conner attempted to call the ranch, but his phone had no reception. He'd wait until they reached the first tall rise and try again. Dallas would be thrilled when she heard the news.

"I'll lead the mare. You take the other two, okay?" he suggested to Javier.

"*Sí,* I follow you."

A good plan. With the mare and colt sandwiched between them, she was less likely to spook and run off. They didn't want to lose her, not after coming this far. The arrangement also helped calm the jittery colt.

A full fifteen minutes passed without incident. Conner was beginning to think they were in the clear. Then they neared the cholla cacti.

How it happened, he wasn't exactly sure, but all at once the colt darted deep into the patch. Surrounded on all sides by dangerous prickles, he instinctively froze.

"Whoa!" Conner dismounted and silently studied their predicament. No easy solution came to him.

The problem was the horses. Unlike at Tom Thumb, there were no trees in the area. Hardly any bushes. Plenty of cacti. How to secure the animals while he went after the colt? Expecting Javier to maintain control of five horses, one of them an anxious mother, was asking a lot. But unless the colt decided to come out on his own, they didn't have much choice.

Javier took the initiative by grabbing the mare's lead rope. "*Ándale.*"

"You sure about this?" Conner asked, regarding the man's small stature.

"Get the baby."

This had better work.

The little fellow trembled as Conner neared, his eyes widening until the whites shone all around.

"Easy does it. Good boy."

The colt made anxious noises, which upset his mother.

Conner moved slowly. With each step he took, he checked

the ground, being careful where he placed his boots. Fallen cholla clusters were everywhere and would attach to him like iron shavings to a magnet.

The closer he got, the more agitated the colt became. No way would he submit to being led out. Conner paused and reconsidered his options. If he circled the animal and came up behind him, the colt might take off running, hopefully in the direction of his mother. He might wind up with a few stickers in his hide, but none the worse for wear.

The colt's eyes were glued on Conner as he executed a wide circle. The animal didn't turn around, but his bobbing head indicated how nervous he was.

Conner was just about in place when a sharp, searing pain exploded in his right elbow.

He swore under his breath, knowing without looking that he'd come in contact with a cholla. A glance confirmed it. The cluster was clinging to his jacket sleeve, the stickers piercing the heavy canvas material as if it were tissue paper.

"Señor Conner, *está bien?*" Javier called through the darkness.

"I'm fine." Conner would have to deal with the cholla after he got the colt. It would be ugly and hurt like hell. "Come on, boy. Make this easy for both of us."

He crept forward, but the colt did no more than swish his stubby tail. After all his antics, he chose now to stand still? Conner hesitated briefly before placing his hand on the animal's rump. This would surely get him moving.

It did, only not in the direction of his mother.

The colt hopped twice on his hind legs like a sprinter revving up for the start of a race. Without warning, he kicked out, planting both back hooves square in the center of Conner's chest. With an angry squeal, he charged out of the cholla patch.

The colt was small, but packed a punch. Conner stumbled, struggling to gather his legs under him. For a second, he thought he'd succeeded, but didn't count on the gopher hole his right heel plunged into.

He toppled backward, landing on a particularly large cholla and crying out as hundreds of stickers pierced his flesh. He vaguely heard Javier call out his name.

Conner didn't move. Not so much as a finger. He didn't dare. He was in serious trouble and the slightest movement would only intensify the pain.

Where was Javier? He must be trying to figure out what to do with the horses.

No tree, no bushes.

Conner was royally screwed.

He gritted his teeth. Seconds dragged by, turning into minutes. He didn't speak. Simply breathing caused enough agony.

Javier's face suddenly appeared above him, floating in the darkness like a helium-filled balloon.

"Help me up," Conner choked out.

"Esto afectará."

"I know it will hurt. Just do it."

Javier grabbed Conner's hands, the only part of his upper body free of cholla stickers. *"Uno, dos, tres, quatro."*

Quatro? How high was he going to count?

"Cinco." Javier pulled.

Conner didn't scream. But the stars twinkling in the night sky were nothing compared to the ones exploding behind his closed eyelids.

Chapter Ten

"Conner! Are you all right?" Dallas hurried toward him as he awkwardly climbed down from his horse, barely beating Gavin.

"Don't come near me," Conner barked through clenched teeth.

She halted in her tracks. What was wrong with her? Of course he didn't want anyone near him. Not with what appeared to be a thousand cholla stickers imbedded in his jacket.

"What can I do to help? Should I call Caitlin?"

Gavin's sister-in-law would know the right treatment. Maybe she'd come over, even though it was well past dinnertime and she and Ethan had an infant at home.

"I don't need a nurse," Conner grumbled. "I can handle this myself."

"Seriously?" She took a tentative step toward him, wincing when she saw the remaining cholla clusters still clinging to him. "And how exactly will that work? You wave a magic wand?"

Javier came over, made a sweeping motion with his hand. "I try to...I use a stick."

Dallas understood that to mean he'd brushed off as many of the clusters as he could. Unfortunately, the cacti's built-in defense was to leave stickers behind. Lots and lots and lots of them.

"What are you doing?" she demanded when Conner started leading his horse away.

"Putting this fellow up for the night and seeing to the mare and colt."

Men! Honestly. Why did they feel it was necessary to always act tough?

"There are plenty of people to do that." She glanced around. In addition to Javier, another wrangler and three late-staying customers had gathered to watch.

"She's right." Gavin relieved Conner of his horse's reins. He already had hold of the injured mare. "You need to look after yourself."

Finally! Someone making sense.

"Go easy with her," Conner warned.

For the first time since he'd ridden into the ranch, Dallas's attention was drawn away from him to the mare and colt.

Though it was too dark to see much, they looked unchanged. No, wait. The faint outline of ribs could be seen on the mare's flanks. And her head drooped, from fatigue and loss of strength. The colt, though active and alert, was also underweight.

Dallas's heart ached.

How fortunate that the pair had been found before winter set in and their odds of survival plummeted.

There had been a cost to the rescue, however. Poor Conner. He had to be suffering.

"Will you call the vet out?" she asked Gavin.

"I already did. He'll be here first thing in the morning."

"Not tonight?"

"He had an emergency."

"This is an emergency, too. Call another vet."

"The mare's survived this long with the arrows," Gavin said reassuringly. "She'll last another twelve hours."

Dallas consoled herself with the knowledge that the mare

and colt would be spending the night in a clean, roomy stall with all the fresh water and food they could consume.

She watched Gavin lead them to the barn, wondering again what kind of cruel individual would intentionally hurt an innocent animal. It was a question she asked repeatedly while volunteering at the animal shelters. Sadly, this wasn't the only, or even the worst, case of abuse she'd seen.

Javier and the other wrangler followed with the remaining horses, including Conner's.

She turned and discovered him walking stiffly in the direction of his apartment. She broke into a run.

"I'm fine, Dallas," he muttered when she reached him.

"You need help. No reason to suffer alone."

To her surprise, he offered no additional protests. Maybe he wasn't so tough, after all.

"Your secret will be safe with me," she said.

"What secret?"

"I won't tell anyone you broke down and cried when the stickers came out."

He stared at her. "You're joking."

"I'm not."

"I'll bite on a wooden spoon."

"Now *you're* joking."

Inside the apartment he flipped on a light switch. The sitting area contained well-worn, hand-me-down furniture from at least three decades ago. In the kitchen, he turned on another light. Someone—Conner?—had added a few homey touches. Pictures near the door. A colorful afghan on the couch. Painted ceramic canisters lined up in a row on the counter.

Dallas could do a lot with the empty white wall behind the TV.

Despite the age and condition of the furnishings, the place was cozy and comfortable and perfectly adequate. It was also small. A third the size of her town house and possibly a sixth the size of Conner's house.

"I know it's not much." He pulled out a chair and sat at the table, careful not to come in contact with anything.

"I like it," she announced. And she did. It suited this Conner, the one who made his living as a ranch hand.

Carefully, he began to peel off his jacket, one inch at a time. His face contorted in agony, though he didn't utter a sound.

"You need that wooden spoon?"

He tried to chuckle but wound up coughing.

"Let me help." She reached for his jacket collar.

"Go slow," he said. "Really slow."

"Maybe we should try fast. Like ripping off a bandage." She felt him tense beneath her hands. "Do it."

"Okay." She readied herself. "Say when."

He drew in a breath and nodded.

She pulled the jacket off his shoulders and down his back. At his wrists, it bunched and refused to budge.

Conner swore ripely.

She half expected him to jump out of his chair. Or faint. That was what she'd have done.

Removing the jacket the rest of the way wasn't nearly as difficult. Thank goodness for small favors. Setting it on the counter to deal with later, she examined his back.

"How bad is it?" he asked, his breathing fast and shallow.

She waited for her voice to return to normal. "Not very."

"You're lying."

"A little."

Every square inch of his back had stickers. His arms and shoulders weren't much better.

He started unbuttoning his shirt.

"Are you ready for this?" she asked doubtfully. The second round would surely hurt as much as the first. "We can wait a little bit."

"I want to get it over with."

That made two of them. Just looking at him was enough to bring tears to her eyes.

They removed his shirt the same way they had his jacket, swiftly and with one tug. Conner didn't swear this time, although his face turned three shades paler.

Dallas examined his bare back. It resembled a bed of nails. "You have to go to the emergency clinic."

"I'll be fine."

"You can't walk around with all these stickers in you." How would he sleep? Train horses? Dress?

"I won't have to. You're going to pull them out."

"Uh-uh. No way!"

Dallas had stepped on cholla before. She knew the barbed tips could penetrate half an inch and be excruciating to remove. Two or three were bad enough. Conner had hundreds.

"I know a trick."

"It had better be good."

He explained the process, which involved snipping the ends of the stickers until only a tiny bit protruded. Then they'd soak his skin with hot towels. When the spines were sufficiently softened, they'd slip right out.

Dallas had her doubts, but fetched scissors from the kitchen drawer. They were old and, in her opinion, unsanitary. "It's not too late to change your mind about the clinic."

He shook his head. "Gavin's dad taught us this when we were in Boy Scouts."

"You must have a long history of getting into trouble."

"I plead the Fifth."

"Hmm." She'd leave that discussion for another day. "Do you have any tweezers?"

"Bathroom medicine cabinet. Clean towels are on the shelf to the right of the sink."

After snipping the stickers, which was quite an operation,

she soaked and then heated the hand towels in the microwave. Exercising tremendous care, she laid the first towel on his arm.

"Too hot?"

"Perfect."

Conner flinched but said nothing when she inadvertently pulled on a sticker.

"Sorry."

"Just keep going."

After she was done arranging the towels, she studied her handiwork. Poor, poor guy.

They chatted while the towels cooled. He told her about capturing the mare and his subsequent run-in with the cactus.

"And that damn colt didn't get a single sticker in him," he finished with a laugh.

She was glad to see Conner's spirits rising.

After repeating the process several times, his shoulders and back were a bright scarlet.

"Try removing one of the stickers."

"Are you positive?" Her hands threatened to tremble at the prospect. "The clinic's open till ten."

"Quit being such a whiner."

"I don't whine. Not a lot."

She took the tweezers and ever so gently tested one sticker. Before she even realized it, the thorn had come out. She went giddy with relief. "It worked!"

"Don't stop."

She kept going, but not every barb cooperated. She left the stubborn ones for later. About three dozen remained when she finished. Much better than hundreds.

"That's amazing."

"Heat more towels."

"How 'bout we take a break?" she suggested. "No offense, but you look like you could use one."

The lines around his mouth had deepened, and his knuckles were still white from clutching the tabletop.

"I want this over with."

Arguing with him was useless.

"You know, you saved that mare and her colt. They wouldn't have lasted much longer."

He hissed as she worked on a particularly deep sticker. "I'd like to think someone else would have found them if we didn't."

"Any ideas where she came from?"

"No. She has a brand on her left hindquarter. I don't recognize it, but maybe Gavin will."

"Are brands registered? Is there any way to research it?"

"They are registered. With the Arizona Department of Agriculture. Of course the horse could be from another state."

Dallas used the tweezers to drop another sticker into the saucer she'd been using to collect them. The amount was staggering.

"What if I take a picture of the brand? Send it to the media as a follow-up."

"It'd probably be faster than contacting the Department of Agriculture."

Finally, the last sticker was out. Dallas wasn't sure which of them breathed the larger sigh.

"We should put some antiseptic on you." She skimmed her fingertips ever so lightly over Conner's inflamed and irritated skin.

"There's a bottle of peroxide in the medicine cabinet."

"That's going to sting."

"Can't be any worse than landing on a cholla." He closed his eyes.

Was it her imagination or did he enjoy her light caresses? As much pain as he had to be in, it couldn't feel good.

And yet he relaxed for the first time all evening, leaning into her fingers. Even his breathing slowed, and the rigid lines around his mouth softened.

This was madness. She couldn't continue stroking him. What was she thinking? What was *he* thinking?

"Nice," he murmured. "Thanks."

There was her answer.

She moved away. "I'll get the peroxide."

While she was in the bathroom, he retrieved a clean T-shirt from the dresser in the sleeping alcove. Not quite a room, the space was separated from the rest of the apartment by a half wall.

An image of the spacious master bedroom at Conner's house came to her. She'd seen it only once, from the doorway. His old girlfriend had taken a group of mostly female guests on a tour during a holiday party.

Did he miss his house?

Did he miss his model ex-girlfriend?

What difference did it make to Dallas one way or the other? She dismissed all thoughts of Conner—for about five seconds. Until he returned to the kitchen, white T-shirt in hand.

She'd never seen him shirtless. Not before tonight, now, without a million cholla spikes distracting her, she took in the defined muscles and trim physique she'd only guessed. She didn't recover until he sat down, his back to her once again.

When she spoke, her voice was thready. "Do you, um, have any cotton balls? For the peroxide."

"Afraid you're going to have to make do with tissues."

She snatched several from the box on the kitchen counter, then uncapped the peroxide.

"Ow, ow, ow!" Conner jerked when she dabbed the antiseptic on his back. "Not so rough."

She snorted. "You let me pull a couple hundred stickers

out of you and didn't make a peep. Yet you complain about a little peroxide."

"I was in shock."

"And now?"

He turned around in the chair, his gaze connecting with hers. "Now I'm not."

Careful, she thought. They were crossing the line again. And it wasn't all Conner's fault. Hadn't she just spent several moments running her fingers over his back for no reason other than it felt nice?

He started to rise, and lifted a hand toward her cheek.

She waited for the electric thrill his touch always elicited, only he hesitated.

They were at the edge. The point of no return. They either acted on their attraction or put a stop to it once and for all.

"Conner, wait. We shouldn't—"

He fell into the chair and scrubbed his palm over his face. "You're right. The timing stinks. For both of us."

"I'm glad you understand."

Was she? A part of her would have liked him to ignore her warning, haul her off her feet and into his arms.

"Come on," she said lightly, and twirled a finger, indicating for him to turn around. "I'm almost done. Oh, and here's some ibuprofen I found in the cabinet."

"Will I see you tomorrow?"

She was coming to the ranch, but would he see her? There was a difference. A big one.

"I'll be here. I want to check on the mare after the vet's treated her, and take some pictures of her brand. I'm not sure when—I have an appointment first. At the doctor's. For a checkup. Richard's taking me."

The reminder of her circumstances had the desired effect. Conner didn't make any more personal remarks. Neither did he walk her to her car, which had to be a first.

This was what she wanted, right? She'd set the boundaries, and he was respecting them.

Why, then, did disappointment consume her and linger long after she arrived home?

CONNER WASN'T AT THE RANCH when Dallas arrived. Considering their uncomfortable parting the previous night, it was just as well, she convinced herself, as she unloaded her camera bag.

Had she made a mistake inviting him to the charity dance? Perhaps. But they were both grown-ups and capable of behaving for one evening. More important, they were friends.

Besides, uninviting him would be an admission of how strong her feelings for him had become these past weeks. Had really always been. Best that remain her little secret.

Richard hadn't helped. While waiting in the doctor's office this morning, he'd asked about her car, which had indeed required a new starter. Then he'd asked about Conner. Dallas had recounted the capture of the mare and colt, along with his fall onto the cholla. She purposely excluded her part in removing the stickers. And she didn't mention the charity dinner, either.

Gavin was outside the mare and colt's stall when she arrived, conversing with an older gentleman in a khaki uniform. A younger man in jeans, boots and a blue work shirt—the veterinarian, she assumed—was with the two horses. A large medical case stood open in a corner.

The mare appeared to be taking all the commotion in stride. Her baby was less enthused and hid behind her, occasionally poking his head out for a quick peek.

The vet was still here after all this time? That was a surprise. Perhaps the mare was worse off than they'd thought.

Dallas was contemplating leaving and coming back later, when Gavin motioned for her to join him and the uniformed man.

"Dallas Sorrenson, this is Agent Ferreras from Game and Fish."

"Nice to meet you." She returned the short, beefy man's handshake.

"If you have a few minutes, I'd like to ask you some questions for our investigation."

"Absolutely. Do you have any leads?" From the corner of her eye, she watched the vet apply a gooey yellow salve to the mare's open wounds.

"Nothing yet. The arrows appear to be standard hunting issue, without specific identifying marks. Ones that could be purchased from any sporting goods store or online. We're sending them to the lab for analysis, but it's going to be waste of time. According to Dr. Schaeffer here, the horse sustained her injuries three to four weeks ago. Any prints or DNA evidence would have long since degraded."

"That's too bad."

"Our best bet—frankly, our only one—is that someone with information is willing to come forward."

"You don't sound hopeful, Agent Ferreras."

"I'm not, I'm sorry to say."

Dallas was sorry, too. She wouldn't give up just yet, however.

"What's most important is the mare and colt are safe and going to recover." She glanced at the vet, and then at Gavin. "She will recover, right?"

"Don't worry. It's not nearly as bad as it looks."

Thank goodness, because it looked terrible.

"Do you have any extra pictures I can have?" Agent Ferreras asked Dallas.

"Not with me, but I can email you some."

He removed a business card from his wallet. "I'd much appreciate that."

"What if I were to take a video of the mare with my phone and upload it to YouTube?"

The man shrugged. "It's worth a shot."

They spent several minutes discussing Dallas's initial encounter with the mare.

"Connor Durham can probably tell you a lot more than me."

"We're waiting for him," Gavin said. "He's on his way."

On his way? She should hurry. She didn't want him thinking she was hanging around in the hopes they'd run into each other. "If you don't need anything else from me, I'd like to take some pictures of the mare's brand."

"Email me a copy of those, too, and I'll see if I can't push through a request with the Department of Agriculture." Agent Ferreras sighed. "They can be mighty slow down there."

"Hard to believe someone could lose a horse."

"Happens more than you think. We retrieve four or five free-ranging horses a year. They get to be quite a nuisance to the ranchers."

With Dr. Schaeffer's permission, Dallas entered the stall and took some close-ups of the brand. It resembled a sideways V with a slash through the center. Gavin and Agent Ferreras left for the office, presumably to wait for Conner.

No one had mentioned where he was, and Dallas refused to inquire.

"Was it difficult removing the arrows?" she asked the vet.

"Not too bad. We had to tranquilize her first before she'd let us near." Dr. Schaeffer had a pleasant smile and he flashed it often. "I'm mostly concerned about infection. Deep wounds like these are slow to heal. She'll be on an antibiotics regimen for weeks, if not months."

The wounds were gruesome. One ragged hole spread six inches across. Dallas steeled herself and took more shots, deciding she would track the mare's healing progress with photographs for as long as she was at Powell Ranch.

"She'll feel a lot better by tomorrow," Dr. Schaeffer said. "In a few weeks, she'll be a brand-new horse."

"What about the colt?"

With less people around, the little fellow had ventured out. At that moment, he had his nose in the vet's medical case, investigating the contents. Dallas took his picture before he scampered away.

"Nothing wrong with him that a few extra groceries and some taming won't fix."

"Conner and Gavin will make sure he gets both."

"The good news is mama and baby are young and strong," the vet continued.

"How old is she?"

"No more than five, I'd say. The colt's about ten months old, judging by his teeth. A little small for his age. I figured him younger at first." Dr. Schaeffer stepped back and assessed them. "I wish she could talk. I'd give anything to know how they survived and where they found water."

"If she could talk, I'd want her to tell us who shot her."

"That, too."

"Is it at all possible to determine how long she was running wild?" Dallas returned her camera to the bag, switched on her cell phone's video function and began filming.

"Can't say for sure." He lifted the mare's front foot. "Judging by the condition of her hooves, I'd estimate over a year. Two, more likely."

"Which means the colt was born in the wild."

"Possibly conceived in the wild." The vet smiled and wiped his hands on a cloth. "Don't suppose we'll ever know."

Conner and Gavin wouldn't approve, but Dallas asked, anyway. "I've got this crazy idea that the colt is Prince's son."

The vet shrugged. "It's not impossible."

"Really?" Someone actually agreed with her?

"They were both loose in the mountains at the same time."

"Now I really wish she could talk."

"We can always run a DNA test."

"There's such a thing for horses?"

"Tests to establish parentage are actually becoming common. I'll talk to Gavin."

"He won't agree. He's convinced Prince isn't the colt's father."

"Don't know why. Prince stole Gavin's wife's horse practically right out from under his nose and bred her."

"True!"

"In fact, I'll use that argument when we talk." Dr. Schaeffer flashed another smile.

"How long until the results come in?" Dallas stopped filming and exited the stall.

"Normally, three to six weeks. But I'll pull some strings." He removed a small zippered plastic bag from his medical case. Cornering the colt, he began removing hairs from the tail. "For the test," he said.

It was a tricky procedure, one the colt clearly resented.

Dallas gave the vet credit; he was brave.

She was about to ask another question when an SUV pulled up and parked just outside the barn door. It bore a logo on the side Dallas couldn't quite make out. Nor did she recognize the uniform the man wore until he got closer.

"Morning, folks." A polar opposite of the Game and Fish agent, this man was tall and reed thin. "Officer Grady with the Arizona Humane Society. I'm here to see Gavin Powell."

"He's in the office," Dallas said. "I can take you there."

His glance cut to the mare. "This her?"

"It is." Dr. Schaeffer met Officer Grady outside the stall, and they discussed the mare at length.

Dallas listened intently without trying to be obvious about it. She was pleased to learn the AHS treated cruelty cases every bit as seriously as the Game and Fish.

"You taking pictures of the mare?" Officer Grady nodded at her camera bag.

"I have been from the day we found her on the mountain."

"You're that gal who sent the photos to the news stations."

"Guilty as charged."

"Good job. You saved two lives." His tone, previously curt, reflected admiration.

Dallas felt her smile blossom. "Thank you."

She *had* done well. And her photos had made a difference. It's what she'd always dreamed of.

Like her mother and father had dreamed of doing when they were young.

"Any chance I can get copies of the pictures you took today?" Officer Grady passed her his business card.

She was acquiring quite a collection. "Absolutely."

After saying goodbye to Dr. Schaeffer, she escorted the officer to where Gavin and Agent Fererras waited. She wasn't asked to stay, which was a shame. She'd have liked to learn more about what steps the agencies were considering.

Then again… She reached for her phone to check the time. Where had the last hour gone? If she hurried, she could grab a quick lunch before her next appointment, head shots for a local businessman.

She was busy composing a mental list of the equipment she'd need and didn't notice Conner until he spoke her name.

"Oh, hi." She stopped just short of her car and stared. Then blinked.

Conner was dressed in a dark gray suit, complete with dress shoes and tie. He looked totally out of place on a horse ranch and absolutely delicious.

She hadn't seen him in a suit before. Dress slacks and a dress shirt, sure, in the days when she'd stopped by Triad's offices to meet with Richard for whatever reason. But not in a suit.

He should wear them more often, she decided. Clothes definitely made the man. Or was it the other way around? He would turn every female head at the charity dinner on Saturday, hers included.

No chance was she uninviting him after this.

"You look great," she blurted without thinking.

He didn't acknowledge the compliment. "Just came from an interview."

"How'd it go?"

"I'm trying not to get my hopes up."

"But you are."

"This job would be a good fit. And I think they liked me."

She could hear the enthusiasm in his voice. She also heard him attempting to suppress it.

"Conner, you're going to find a job. You're too talented and too smart to be without one for long."

"Gavin phoned me. Said to come to the office the minute I got back."

"An agent from the Game and Fish and an officer from the Arizona Humane Society are in there. They want to ask you some questions."

"All right. I'll catch up with you later."

"Have to be much later. I've got a busy afternoon."

He nodded and started around the corner to the barn entrance, his steps lacking any spring.

She suddenly remembered and called out, "How's your back?"

"Fine."

She believed him. It was his insides that hurt, and there was nothing she or anyone could do to help.

Chapter Eleven

For the third time this week, Conner tucked his dress shirt into his trousers, straightened the knot in his tie and shoved his arms into a suit jacket. But instead of going on an interview, he was escorting Dallas to the AAWA charity dinner.

It wasn't a date. He'd reminded himself of the fact enough times over the last several days and it had finally sunk in. That he hadn't seen her since the morning after they'd captured the mare and colt made it easier.

The same day he'd interviewed at the metal fabrication company. Another job he didn't get.

According to Gavin, Dallas had been to the ranch once since then to take more pictures. Her determination was admirable. If anyone could find the mare's owner or the person responsible for shooting her, it would be Dallas.

Conner missed her. Not a day or an hour passed that he didn't recall the touch of her gentle hands skimming his naked back. He'd say the excruciating pain of the cholla cactus was well worth it, but...

Who was he kidding? Hell, yes, it was worth it.

And that was why any romantic thoughts of her needed to stop.

Whatever decisions she and Richard reached, regarding the baby and the future of their relationship, would be made without Conner in the picture.

He tried remembering how much gas was in his truck and decided he had enough. It wasn't too often he wished he still owned his convertible. Tonight, he did. Picking up Dallas in his weathered old Ford, imagining them pulling up to valet parking at the fancy resort, was enough to ruin his mood—which wasn't that good to begin with.

At the door to his apartment he paused, his hand itching to grab his cowboy hat from the peg where it hung. *No crutches,* he silently vowed, and left without it.

"Hooo, doggie." A familiar form reclined against the side of Conner's truck, a Stetson pulled low over his brow. "If you looked any prettier, I'd take you out myself."

That brought a smile to Conner's face for the first time all day. "Hey, Clay. A little late for you to be out, isn't it?"

His friend had been keeping much earlier hours since getting married and becoming a father.

"I had an errand to run. This." He tossed something at Conner.

Instinctively grabbing for the flying object, Conner caught it in midair. The car keys jangled in his hands. "What's this?"

"I figured you could use a different set of wheels tonight."

Puzzled, Conner walked a few steps, just far enough to see Clay's BMW parked on the other side of his truck.

He grabbed hold of his emotions before they colored his voice. "You're lending me your car?"

"Can't expect a pregnant woman wearing an evening dress and heels to ride in this hunk of junk."

Conner didn't know when he'd appreciated a friend more. "Thanks, buddy."

Clay hooked a friendly arm around his neck, as he'd often done when they were teenagers. "No rush getting the car back. I don't need it till Monday."

"Be sure and give Sierra my best."

"I will." He grinned stupidly. "We're having another baby.

Just found out yesterday. She took one of those home pregnancy tests."

"Congratulations." Conner pulled him into a back-slapping bear hug.

"We're happy." He looked it.

For a brief moment, Conner was jealous. He'd been that happy once.

"I'd better hit the road. Bring that boy of yours around for a ride. Isa's old swayback needs more of a workout."

"Sierra would skin me alive."

"You don't have to tell her."

Clay chuckled. "I don't know how, but she has some sort of built-in GPS when it comes to that kid. I can't even sneak him into the hardware store without her figuring it out. Hate to think how she's going to react the first time I sign him up for a Little Buckaroo Rodeo."

"I'll run interference for you."

"I'll need it."

Conner handed over his keys so Clay could drive his truck home. "Thanks again."

"Enjoy yourself."

That was Conner's problem. He was afraid he was going to enjoy himself too much.

When Dallas greeted him at her front door, she took one look at the car and gave him a startled glance. "Where'd you get that?"

Conner had difficulty answering her. His senses had overloaded his brain, causing it to short circuit.

The dress emphasized every womanly curve, which Dallas had in abundance. Her hair, half up and half down, framed her face in loose waves. She smelled like—he didn't know what, only that he wanted to drown in it.

Which he did when he pulled her into his arms and inhaled deeply.

She laughed into his neck. "Hello to you, too."

"Clay," he said.

"What?" She drew back, her hands resting lightly on his shoulders.

"It's Clay's car. He lent it to me."

"That was sweet of him."

Conner studied her. "You look…" He swallowed. "Incredible."

She studied him in turn. "You look incredible, too. Very handsome."

He was glad she approved. He'd wanted to do right by her, knowing how important this dinner was to her career. "You ready?"

She fetched her wrap and a tiny purse that couldn't possibly contain more than her cell phone, driver's license and a house key.

At the car, Conner held the door open for her. Whatever Clay's real motives were, he'd been right about Dallas. Slipping into the sedan was far easier than crawling into a truck.

They talked easily on the drive to the resort. As the valet drove off with the car, Conner took her arm and led her along the lit walkway to the main entrance. Greeters stationed just inside pointed them in the direction of the ballroom.

They were only a few minutes late, but the room was almost completely full. Locating two empty seats at a table along the far wall, Dallas deposited her wrap.

"I think I'm hungry," she said, eyeing the lengthy buffet loaded with every kind of food imaginable.

It wasn't like Conner to keep a lady waiting. "I could eat a bite."

They navigated the room, with Dallas stopping frequently to say hello to someone and chat briefly. Conner responded cordially when she introduced him as her "friend." By the time they reached the buffet line, he'd forgotten more names than he remembered.

"Champagne?"

Waiters crisscrossed the room carrying heavily laden drink trays.

Dallas patted her stomach. "I think I'm going to stick with water. But you have some."

"I'm good with water, too." He had a one-drink-when-driving rule. He amended that to a *no*-drink-when-driving-a-pregnant-woman-home rule.

They met more people Dallas knew while returning to their table with their plates. Conner admired her poise and confidence. Those individuals she hadn't worked with quickly learned about her photography business when she seamlessly slipped in a reference.

According to Conner's estimation, she'd made five new contacts in the thirty minutes since their arrival.

Maybe he should ask her for lessons. His networking skills were clearly lacking or he'd have found a new job by now.

He'd become complacent at Triad, assuming he'd be there for life. Researching potential jobs was easy, registering with headhunters a necessary evil. His letters of introduction and résumé were evidently written well enough that he was regularly called in for interviews. When it came to closing the deal, however, he continually missed the mark.

The woman sitting on Conner's right dabbed her mouth with a white linen napkin. "The dressing on this endive salad is divine."

To him, salad was salad. But he didn't want to be impolite. "It is good." He took a bite to show his sincerity.

"I don't believe we've met. Have you attended any AAWA events before?"

Because Dallas was deep in conversation with the elderly

couple beside her, Conner turned his full attention to the woman. "My first time."

"They put on a lovely affair. And the money they raise benefits so many worthy causes. If you're here, you must be an animal lover."

"Yes, ma'am."

She extended a hand. The diamond ring on her finger, though large, was tasteful. "I'm Sunday Givens. Nice to meet you."

Something about her short-cropped silver hair and unusual name rang a bell with Conner, but he couldn't quite place her. "Conner Durham."

"You strike me as a dog person. Am I right?"

Conner and his ex-girlfriend had owned an Australian shepherd mix that she got custody of when they split. Much as he'd liked that dog, he hadn't objected. Her daughter was quite attached to "Zero," and he hated to separate them.

"You're correct. Had a lot of good ones in my life. Mostly herding dogs. Dad believed even the family pets should earn their keep."

"You grew up on a ranch?" Sunday took tiny spoonfuls of her lobster bisque.

Conner tried not to wolf his down. "In Mustang Valley."

"And now?"

"Still there."

"That's horse country. How many do you own?"

"None, technically." Another reminder of his circumstances he chose not to dwell on. He'd sold his two quarter horses a few months back, even though Gavin had offered to board them for free. The extra money had come in handy and enabled him to make a few payments on his house. "I'm a trainer. I work for the Powells."

Sunday's attractively crinkled face lit up. "I'm familiar with their mustang sanctuary. Anyone involved with the AAWA is, naturally. They've done some tremendously good things for wild mustangs." She looked at Conner with renewed interest and something he hadn't seen much lately. Respect. "Tell me all about it."

"I'd hate to bore you."

"You won't. I adore cowboys and their way of life. In my opinion, it's becoming a lost art."

Talking with her wasn't hard at all. She asked a lot of questions and encouraged Conner to go into detail when he would have skimmed.

At some point, Dallas must have become aware of them, and joined in on the discussion. "He's been helping me with the book."

"What book is that?"

Dallas explained.

"I'm impressed." Again, Sunday's eyes shone with respect.

"I haven't done that much," Conner insisted.

"Don't listen to him." Dallas laid her hand on his arm and leaned in closer. "There's no way I would have gotten all the photographs I did without him."

"Rest assured, I'm not listening." Sunday's smile alighted on Conner. "Anyone can see he's very unassuming."

"Did he tell you about the wounded mare and colt we found in the mountains?"

"I heard about it on the news. That was you?"

While the waitstaff swooped in to remove empty plates and bowls, Dallas recounted the story, including Conner's encounter with the cholla, and ending with their ongoing efforts to locate the owner.

From the way she told it, she made Conner out to be some kind of hero, which he wasn't. He should warn her to stop laying it on so thick.

"How fortunate you came along when you did," Sunday gushed.

"I really hope they find the person who shot her," Dallas said, "but there's not much chance of it."

"Tell me, Conner, where did you learn to train horses?"

It took him a moment to realize Sunday was speaking to him. "I started out rodeoing."

"A man of many talents."

"He's actually a systems analyst."

He sent Dallas a look meant to silence her. She didn't take the hint.

"He used to work for Triad Energy Systems. Ran their production department."

"I heard they had a major layoff last spring." Sunday's expression was sympathetic. "Were you by chance one of their casualties?"

Conner hesitated before answering. He preferred not advertising his unemployment to strangers. But Sunday impressed him as being nonjudgmental. "Unfortunately, yes."

"A shame. I'm sure you found another job straight away."

"Actually, I'm still looking."

"And training mustangs while you're at it."

"Yes, ma'am."

"Interesting." She pushed her half-eaten cheesecake aside. "As it so happens, we're looking for a good systems analyst at the plant."

"Plant?"

"Sonoran Bottling."

All at once the pieces flew together, and he remembered where he'd seen her—on the cover of countless local business magazines and journals. She was *the* Sunday Givens, president of the most successful independently owned bottling plant in the entire Southwest.

"Call me Monday morning," she said casually, as if she hadn't just changed Conner's entire life, "and we'll set up an interview. If you have a pen and paper, I'll give you my number."

He slapped the front of his jacket, beneath which his heart beat like a piston. "Somewhere here—"

Beside him, Dallas magically produced a pen from her tiny purse.

"Thank you, ma'am." He scribbled Sunday's number on the back of the program agenda. "I really appreciate the opportunity."

She smiled warmly. "No need to be so formal. I consider every employee at Sonoran to be a part of my family."

"SHE'S GOING TO GIVE YOU the job!" Dallas beamed at Conner as they danced to a slow number.

"We'll see."

This was the first opportunity they'd have to talk privately, and she was bursting with excitement.

"She said, and I quote, 'I consider *every* employee at Sonoran to be a part of my family.'" Dallas pinched his chin between her thumb and finger as if to shake some sense into him. "Have faith."

"She did say 'every.'" He finally let his guard down and smiled. "I liked her."

"And she liked you. See? It's kismet."

"Guess I have you to thank." He gazed at Dallas, his expression intimate. Personal.

Chills danced up her spine. "Nonsense."

"If you hadn't dragged me here, I wouldn't have met Sunday."

"All it takes is a connection. I've learned when courting new clients that they're more likely to sign with me if we share an interest. With you and Sunday, it's your mutual love of animals."

They floated across the floor to the music of the string

quartet. She reveled in the new and exciting sensation of his strong hand resting on the small of her back and the breadth of his muscled shoulders beneath her arm.

Then again, she'd felt all that before, and more, when he'd kissed her on her front porch.

"I don't want her giving me the job just because she admires my work with the mustang sanctuary."

"Why not?"

"I want the job because I'm the most qualified candidate."

"Conner, you are the most qualified. You and ten or twenty other applicants. There's always that one thing that makes a person stand out from the rest. It doesn't have to be professional—it can be personal. She thinks it's cool that you train wild mustangs. Take advantage of it. I guarantee you, the other applicants won't hesitate to do the same."

"How'd you get so smart?" He twirled her in a circle. "They teach you that at photography school?"

"I think I picked it up from years of living with Hank."

"I guess growing up with him for a stepdad wasn't all bad."

Something shifted inside her. "No, I guess it wasn't." After another turn on the dance floor, she said, "Call me right away after you talk to Sunday. And take the job when she offers it to you."

"If she offers it."

"When," Dallas reiterated.

"Whatever you say." He dipped her, then pulled her up hard against him.

Dallas's heart cartwheeled. Any reminders about not becoming involved with him were ignored. She was falling fast and with no net in sight.

"Excuse me," Conner said when they bumped into another couple just as the song was ending.

"Conner Durham?" Recognition illuminated the woman eyes. "It's Anita. From Signatures Studio."

"Anita!" He gave the elegantly dressed, middle-aged woman a brief hug. "Good to see you."

"This is my husband." She took the arm of the man beside her.

Names were exchanged as they left the dance floor. At the edge, out of the way of other dancers, they stopped to chat.

"Anita is a friend of Leeza's," Conner explained to Dallas.

"A coworker, actually," Anita amended. "I'm the office manager at the modeling agency where Leeza's registered."

"Oh, okay." A banal reply, but Dallas didn't know how to respond. Conner rarely mentioned his former girlfriend.

Was that because she'd hurt him? Or did he still care?

"Leeza's one of our most requested models." Anita glanced at Dallas and quickly changed the subject. "Where are you working now, Conner?"

He told them about the mustang sanctuary and his work with Dallas. They must have been impressed, because they couldn't take their eyes off him.

Dallas fumed just a tiny bit. She had no reason whatsoever to be jealous. None at all. Just because Leeza was a statuesque model with a runway-worthy figure. After having a child, no less. And was the agency's most requested model.

"Well, we'd best get back to our table," Anita said when a couple brushed by them. "Before we cause an accident."

She and Conner hugged again. He acknowledged her husband with a friendly nod before they parted.

At their table, Dallas grabbed her bag. "If you don't mind, I need to freshen up a bit."

"Can I get you anything while you're gone? Coffee? More water?"

Was the prospect of a job with Sonoran Bottling responsible for the smile on his face? Or was he thinking of Leeza?

"I'm fine, thanks."

Just as Dallas finished washing her hands at the restroom sink, Anita entered.

"Guess we had the same idea," she exclaimed warmly, her gaze traveling to Dallas's waistline. "When are you due?"

The question threw her. She had only just started to show, was at that stage where she could easily be mistaken for carrying a few extra pounds. This was the first time a stranger had noticed her pregnancy.

She felt herself glowing.

"How did you know?" Her hand went automatically to her stomach.

"That," Anita said, smiling sentimentally. "It's something pregnant mothers can't help doing."

Dallas liked being referred to as a pregnant mother. "I'm not due till April 4. Seems like a long way away."

"The weeks will fly by." Anita removed her lipstick from her purse and applied a fresh coat, gazing into the mirror. "Conner's going to be a great dad."

"H-he's not the father." At Anita's confused look, she clarified, "We're just friends. He escorted me here as a favor. I thought it would be a good opportunity for him to make some contacts."

"My mistake." The other woman appeared flustered. "When I saw the two of you dancing...I just assumed."

"There's nothing romantic between us."

"Too bad."

"No, it's good, actually. We've been friends a long time. I wouldn't want to complicate things."

"I meant too bad he's not going to be a father. Conner loves children. He treated Leeza's daughter like his own."

"He did?" Dallas was more than interested; she was fascinated.

"Absolutely. The poor darling was devastated when her mother and Conner broke up. Still is, from what Leeza has said." Anita shook her head. "I tell you, that woman didn't know what she gave up when she walked out. Men like him don't come around often."

"I've seen Conner with his niece. His best friend's step-daughter, actually."

What sort of father would Richard be? He wanted to marry her and was more than willing to provide for their baby. But he generally avoided the company of children and had wanted to wait to start a family.

She would ask him how he really felt if she wasn't convinced he'd say what he thought she wanted to hear.

"What a dolt I am." Anita flushed. "Here I am, going on and on about Conner. I'm sure your husband is every bit as wonderful with kids."

"I'm not married."

She didn't miss a beat. "Your baby's father. He must be thrilled."

"We're not together." As nice as Anita was being, Dallas was starting to feel uncomfortable. She would have made an excuse to leave, but Anita had other ideas.

"I know you said you and Conner aren't dating, but you might reconsider it." When another woman entered the rest-room, Anita lowered her vice to a conspiratorial whisper. "He likes you. I can tell by the way he said your name when he introduced us. Like it melted on his tongue."

Had he really?

"Think about it."

"I...I can't."

Anita smiled saucily. "Sure you can."

Dallas sought Conner out the moment she returned to the banquet room.

Maybe she'd been wrong all along about blended families. Maybe some did work. Gavin and Sage's obviously did. As had Conner and Leeza's. For a while. Her own blended family might have meshed better if Dallas and her brother had given Hank half a chance.

When she reached the table, Conner was wearing an ear-to-ear grin.

"Did something happen while I was gone?"

"Sunday left. She reminded me she'll be waiting for my call Monday morning."

"I have a good feeling about her and the bottling plant, Conner."

"Me, too." He held Dallas's chair for her, ran his fingertips along her bare shoulder, familiarly and affectionately, as if they were indeed a couple.

When he asked her a short while later if she was ready to leave or wanted to dance again, Dallas chose the latter—just so she could enjoy floating in his embrace once more.

It had been an altogether perfect evening. By the time they left, Dallas was more than ready to throw caution to the wind. If Conner tried to kiss her, she'd let him.

And if he didn't, she just might try and kiss *him*.

Chapter Twelve

Conner walked Dallas to her front door. He didn't expect a repeat of the previous time—Richard showing up unexpectedly *or* the kiss. Despite the chemistry between them, she'd given Conner no indication whatsoever that she wanted to be more than friends and business associates.

A shame. She really rocked that dress.

A hug would be appropriate, he decided while she unlocked her door, and not out of line. He reached for her with open arms, only to find himself holding empty air.

She stood on the threshold. "Would you like to come in for a bit? I can fix you a cup of coffee, or maybe you'd like a beer?"

Come in? For a bit? "Yeah, sure. Just a cold drink if you have one."

"Soda or iced tea?"

"Either's fine." He stepped into her town house, watching as she set her bag on an entry table and punched a code into the security alarm pad on the wall. The earsplitting screeching came to an immediate stop.

"Ouch!"

He looked down to find a small white cat clinging to his pant leg. Conner was afraid to move for fear the pinlike nails piercing his skin would go deeper. He'd learned his lesson with the cholla cactus.

"Sorry." Dallas bent and took hold of the tiny, fur-covered terror. "This is Snow White. She likes to play."

"Play?" Conner would hate to be in the cat's way if she was mad.

"Don't move."

"Not a problem."

Dallas gently pried the cat loose and it promptly turned on her. Okay, not turned on her. What he'd mistaken for aggression was actually affection. Wedging herself in the crook of Dallas's neck, Snow White purred, loudly enough to disturb the people sleeping in the unit next door.

"She's a rescue animal," Dallas explained, stroking the cat's back. "I've only had her a couple of months. We're still working on her social skills. She's young and thinks everyone wants to play."

"It figures, the first time I meet her I'm not wearing boots."

Dallas laughed. "Do you like cats?"

"My mom and sisters always had them." He gave Snow White's head a scratching, which revved up her purring. "They always seemed to like me more than I liked them."

"I can see why." Something not quite definable flashed in Dallas's eyes. "You have nice hands."

His pulse instantly spiked. That was definitely not a friends-only signal.

She turned away, making him wonder if he'd misread her. "Over here's Sleeping Beauty."

One of those carpeted cat condos stood in the corner of the room. On the top perch, a hugely fat, striped cat slumbered. It didn't even crack an eye open when Dallas set the little white cat on a lower perch.

"I've had her three years. She was my first rescue. I'd love to have a dog, but my schedule's too hectic. Cats are easier."

Dallas led the way to the kitchen, where she produced two

cans of diet soda from the fridge, offering one to Conner. "Would you like a glass and some ice for that?"

"Don't bother." He popped the top on the can and took a swallow. "It's nice to meet the family."

"Oh, that's not everyone."

On cue, a dusty-gray cat appeared from around the corner. Seeing Dallas, he ran for her, meowing like crazy.

"This is Charming." Dallas stood at the counter while the cat wove around her legs in a continual figure eight pattern. "He's the lover of the bunch."

"I see that."

The cat abruptly stopped, gave Conner a rather disdainful once-over, hissed, and then resumed lavishing affection on Dallas.

"Apparently he's only charming with you."

Dallas frowned in puzzlement. "That's odd. He's usually friendly."

"He must not like the suit."

"Well, I like it." She smiled, that undefinable emotion twinkling in her eyes again.

Conner distracted himself with another swallow of soda. "You have any other cats waiting to pounce on me?"

"Three's my limit. And I only adopted Snow White because she was on the euthanasia list at the county pound. A friend contacted me and asked me to foster her. Temporarily. You can see how that's going."

"Helping animals is your passion. I admire you. I'd have been surprised if you didn't have a houseful of pets."

"Glad to know I didn't disappoint."

Conner had the impression he'd passed some sort of test.

"Sit?" She moved toward the table.

He beat her to it and pulled out her chair.

"You don't have to do that," she insisted. "We're not at the Phoenician anymore."

"My mom was a stickler for manners. Drilled them into me and my sisters at an early age."

"Give her my regards. She did a good job." Dallas waited for him to join her before saying, "I admire you, too."

"For my manners?" He removed his suit jacket and slung it over the back of his chair.

"For making the best of lousy circumstances. The last six months can't have been easy for you. A lot of people would have buckled under, collected unemployment compensation, let the bank repossess their house. You didn't. You're a fighter."

Few people spoke frankly to Conner about the financial ramifications of being laid off. They preferred to tiptoe around the subject for fear of embarrassing or offending him. Her praise for his efforts to salvage what pride he had left made him feel good—confident and capable—when nothing else had lately.

"That means a lot to me."

"Things will be different starting Monday. Your life is about to change."

"Sunday Givens and the Sonoran Bottling Plant." He could still hardly believe it.

"Are you going to quit working with the wild mustangs?"

"I haven't gotten the job yet."

"Don't think like that!"

She was right. He had to be more positive. "No, I'd like to stay involved with the sanctuary, if only on my days off."

She nodded.

He felt as if he'd passed another test. "I owe you."

"Me? You're the one who impressed Sunday."

"You've pushed me. Cheered me on. Encouraged me. Not just through pep talks but by setting an example. The longer I've been away from the corporate world, the harder it is for me to put myself out there."

"You bring a lot to the table, Conner. Professionally and

personally. Anita told me tonight that Leeza made a big mistake leaving you. I agree with her."

"Leeza wanted different things from our relationship."

"Leeza didn't love you. Not enough and not like you deserve to be loved."

"I might have dodged a bullet with her."

"Might have?" Dallas smiled brightly, then shyly. "I won't say I'm unhappy you're single again."

That was all it took. Desire hit Conner with the force of a head-on collision. He wanted her. Like no other woman before. Wanted her so desperately, he couldn't be trusted alone with her a moment longer.

"It's getting late." He stood, his legs weak at the knees, and removed his jacket from the chair. "I should leave."

"All right." She walked with him to the living room. Before they reached the door, she stopped him with a hand on his arm and a soft, "Wait."

"Did I forget something?"

"Only this." She lifted her lips to his and brushed them lightly across his mouth. "I've been wanting to do that all night."

Fire exploded inside him. He dropped his jacket, grabbed her by the shoulders and held her in place against him. "If I kiss you back, I won't stop there."

"Do you want to kiss me back?"

He groaned. "You have no idea."

"I think I do." She placed her palm on his cheek, angled her body closer to his and inhaled as if she couldn't get enough of him.

Before tonight, Conner hadn't considered himself good enough for Dallas. It wasn't just the potential job with Sonoran Bottling that had him reconsidering. It was her belief in him.

"Kiss me," she said, her eyes closing in anticipation. "I want to taste you."

He abandoned all control. Covering her mouth with his, he let the fire burning inside him consume them both.

DALLAS'S HANDS FRAMED Conner's face as he encircled her waist and took possession of her. They fit perfectly, their closeness generating an incredible heat.

She moaned, curled her fingers into the hair at the base of his neck. His body, highly responsive to her every move, went rigid.

Did she have any idea what she was getting into? He anchored her hips to him so there would be no doubt.

Gasping softly, she pulled away. "Give me a second."

He was coming on too strong. Scaring her off. "Dallas, I—"

She kicked off one shoe, then the other. "Much better."

Much better indeed.

They found each other again and kissed hungrily. His hand snaked underneath her dress and skimmed her smooth thigh.

"Mmm." She pushed more material aside.

It was an invitation he couldn't refuse. His fingers climbed till they found the edge of her panties, where they toyed with the elastic leg band.

"Take this off," she murmured, tugging at his tie.

"Let me." The tie landed on the floor beside his jacket.

She undid the top two buttons of his shirt, revealing the patch of hair above the V-neck of his undershirt. Smiling with delight, she lightly caressed him, her nails scraping his fevered skin.

Conner was quickly approaching the point where going back would be impossible. He called on the one tiny sliver of responsibility that remained. "We don't have to do this. It's up to you."

"Make love to me. Please. It's what I want and what I think you want, too."

He did want it. With an intensity that stripped his emotions to their very core.

"What about the baby?"

"The baby will be fine. As long as you're gentle."

"I won't hurt you. Either of you." He'd die first.

She undid two more buttons. His arms shook from the effort of restraining himself.

"There's something you need to know. Before this goes any further." He gulped air, feeding his starving lungs. "I… care about you."

Conner's feelings were more complicated than that, but he wasn't ready to express them. As it was, he could hardly form simple sentences.

"I know. If I didn't, I wouldn't have asked you inside, much less into my bedroom." She grinned wickedly. "Unless you'd rather make love right here on the living room floor."

He bent and lifted her in his arms.

She laughed, light and melodious. The sound galvanized him.

"The bedroom. For the first time. After that, I'll make love to you anywhere in the house. Any room, on any piece of furniture. As many times as you want."

Her brows rose. "I just might take you up on that."

Now it was his turn to grin wickedly. "Which way?"

He carried her down the hall and into the master bedroom. Enough light shone in for him to make out the bed. He headed straight for it.

He set Dallas down on the mattress, following her as she lay back on the quilted spread, arms stretched over her head. She looked like a dream in the pale, pale light. Sensuous and alluring.

"You're incredible." He reached for her dress, slipping it slowly up her thighs.

"Wait one minute." She stayed his hand.

"Is something wrong?"

"You first," she said quietly, lowering her eyes.

Was she shy? She hadn't been till now.

"It's okay," he murmured.

"Easy for you to say. Your body isn't changing on you every day. Becoming rounder and softer and…different."

"I like rounder and softer and different."

"Yeah. Okay."

He tilted her chin until her gaze met his. "You're beautiful, Dallas, and sexy as hell."

"I still want you to go first."

"Gladly." He released her and yanked his dress shirt and undershirt from the waistband of his trousers. His belt came next. Then his boots and socks.

"Let me."

Rising onto her knees, she removed his dress shirt, peeling it off him much like the night in his apartment when she helped him with the cholla stickers. With one barrier gone, she let her fingers glide over his biceps, murmuring admiringly. Finally, she removed his undershirt, sliding it over his head and tossing it aside. Her eyes sparked, reflecting her appreciation as they traveled down his naked torso, and then turned dark.

She sighed. "I can't not touch you."

The sensation of her fingers on his chest was like warm silk. Her lips, dropping light kisses in the wake of her fingers, seared his skin.

"I want to go slow." She returned to his mouth, covered it with hers.

What she wanted to do was kill him by slow torture.

He unfastened his trousers. She unzipped them. Her hand made contact with his erection through his briefs. A current of pure electricity shot through him.

"Dallas, I…" She wasn't making this easy. "I don't have any condoms. Wasn't planning on this. Us."

She swept his hair from his eyes, the gesture tender. "It's a little late to worry about birth control."

"Not that. I'm healthy. I promise. But you shouldn't take any risks. Not with the baby."

"Thank you for being considerate. I have some. Left over—"

"Where?"

"In the nightstand."

He opened the drawer and found enough packets that they could try out two more places besides the bed, if Dallas had the inclination and he the strength.

He hastily removed his trousers and briefs. Naked at last, he stood before her.

She lowered herself onto her calves and stared. With each passing second, he grew harder.

"You're beautiful," she breathed.

A lifetime of sports, rodeoing and breaking horses had left their marks on him, good and bad. He hoped his toned muscles made a better impression than his scars.

Evidently so. She skimmed her fingers over his stomach, let them drift upward through the hair on his chest. Stopping over his heart, she laid her palm flat and exhaled slowly.

"Dallas." He placed his hand atop hers, incapable of saying more than her name. For several moments, they didn't move.

"I want you, Conner," she whispered. "Do you understand?"

He did. Because he wanted her to the very center of the heart both their hands covered.

"Show me," he told her.

She reached for his erection.

"No. Not that. Show me *you*."

After a moment, she nodded and presented her back to him. "Unzip me."

He did, his fingers fumbling.

The slinky dress came away, like the petals of a flower opening to the sun.

She wore some sort of one-piece bra and panty combo that was made of the sheerest material Conner had ever seen. It left little—and everything—to the imagination. He wasn't sure he wanted her to take it off.

Then she did, squirming out of it in a seductive dance that sent his blood coursing through his veins.

When she finished, she sat on the bed before him, her legs tucked under her, every vulnerable and voluptuous inch of her exposed.

"You're mine," he said.

"Always."

He wasn't certain which one of them moved first. At the same moment Dallas drew him down onto the mattress, he covered her body with his, their mouths meeting in a hungry kiss, his hands already roaming.

She arched, shifted, opened herself to him, and he committed every touch, every sound, every taste of her to memory. Her tiny moans and gasps of excitement were like a magic elixir, healing the ragged tears in his soul and making him whole again.

He groaned when her fingers skimmed his ribs, and then cupped his buttocks. Lifting her hips, she rubbed herself against him. He shot like a rocket straight to the edge.

She let go of him and reached for the condom.

"Not yet." Speaking required tremendous effort.

"You're ready."

"You're not."

He brought his head to her breasts, filled his hands with the pliant mounds and teased the nipples with his teeth and tongue.

She moaned, and her head collapsed onto the pillow.

"Am I hurting you?"

"Yes. No. I'm tender." Another low moan escaped her. "Just keep doing what you're doing."

He was happy to, until temptation won over. Starting in the sensitive valley between her breasts, he forged a path of damp kisses that ended at her rounded tummy.

She jerked and tried to push him away.

"What's wrong?"

"I'm not…my belly isn't flat anymore."

"Your belly is gorgeous." He splayed his hand across it and let it remain until she relaxed. "Don't think otherwise."

"I can't help being self-conscious."

"There isn't anything about you or your body that isn't a complete and total turn-on for me."

His hand ventured to where her legs joined, and parted them. Carefully, then with increased vigor, he stroked her moist center, first with his fingers, then his mouth. He was more than content to satisfy her this way for as long as she wanted. Till she came apart.

She writhed, trembled, and he sensed she was nearing her peak. Suddenly, she grabbed his arms and drew him up until they were once again face-to-face.

"I want you inside me."

Who was he to disappoint her?

Sheathing himself in the condom, he entered her slowly. She wrapped her legs around his middle.

"Are you absolutely sure?"

"Very." She arched into him, urging him on.

"Look at me." He thrust deeper, but still slowly.

She did look, and when she saw him, really saw him, he increased his momentum. Her climax was swift and complete and stunning to watch. Only when she started to return to him did he let go. She was still trembling with aftershocks when he buried himself deep in her one last time, the force of his release leaving him weak.

He fell on his side next to her, his heart beating like a giant fist pounding his chest.

"Are you okay? No pain?"

"I'm a whole lot more than okay." She rolled toward him, snuggled into him and flung an arm over his middle. "I'm exactly where I should be."

"You are." He wasn't referring to her bed or in his embrace. He hoped she knew that. "I want to see you again."

"You will."

"I'm talking about a date. Movies, a concert. Not at the ranch, when you happen to be stopping by for work."

"If you insist."

He felt her smile against his neck. "Tomorrow?"

"I'm having dinner at my parents'."

"I like your parents."

"Are you trying to wrangle an invitation to dinner?" She propped herself up on one elbow to stare pointedly at him.

"Am I succeeding?"

"I'm sure Mom will be delighted."

"It'll give me an opportunity to thank your stepdad for his help."

"Luckily, you don't need any more contacts." She pressed a kiss to his lips, let her tongue trace the outline. "Since you're going to be Sonoran Bottling's newest systems analyst."

Conner didn't correct her as he'd been doing. He was applying her advice and thinking positively. It had worked great the last hour.

"Tired?" he asked.

Her fingers were painting lazy patterns on his chest and her eyes, he noticed, had drifted closed.

"No, content."

She sounded it.

"It's late. I don't want to keep you up."

Her eyes snapped open. "Are you tired?"

"Not at all." If anything, he was energized.

"Good." She pushed him onto his back and slid her body onto his so they were once again heart to heart.

Conner approved of the change.

Her hands, ever curious, went on a mission to completely familiarize themselves with him. Any residual shyness was completely gone. He was starting to anticipate where things were going to lead when an unexpected visitor plunked down onto the bed right beside them.

Conner turned his head, only to encounter two golden eyes and an angry hiss. Charming, apparently upset that there was an intruder in his personal territory, was displaying his less than charming side.

"Sorry." Dallas tried to dislodge the cat and send him on his way.

The little beast would have none of it, turning himself into a solid and unmovable object. Then, with another small thunk, Snow White appeared. She instantly started swatting Charming's tail, which twitched angrily.

Conner decided he liked the dozing Sleeping Beauty best of all of Dallas's cats.

"Honestly," she complained, giving Charming another push. "I can't figure out what's gotten into him."

"It's all right. They can have the bed." Conner swung his legs onto the floor. Grabbing her hand, he hauled her to her feet. "We can go elsewhere."

"Like?" Her smile grew.

"Wherever you want."

They ended up in the shower, where they played beneath the water's spray. Afterward, wrapped in towels, their hair still wet, they padded to the living room. His target was the couch. Hers was the rug in front of the unlit fireplace. He let her choose.

When he next came over, Conner thought, he'd bring wood

and light a fire, then make love to her in the golden glow of the flames.

Tomorrow, perhaps. After dinner with her parents.

For the first time in a very long time, Conner's future contained endless and exciting possibilities.

And it was all because of Dallas.

Chapter Thirteen

Dallas gripped the steering wheel of her Prius so tightly her fingers cramped. Would the darn stoplight ever change to green? When it finally did, she hit the gas, wishing for once she owned an eco-*un*friendly fuel guzzler with decent get-up-and-go.

In her favor, there were only stop signs between here and Powell Ranch. She wanted to arrive before the elderly gentleman in order to capture his expression on film when he saw the mare and colt for the first time.

Hard to believe someone had finally stepped forward after nearly two weeks, claiming not only to have information on the mare but to be her owner. According to Conner, the man had pictures and registration papers to prove it. She'd be interested in seeing them.

Along with everyone else, she'd become attached to the horses and had an emotional stake in their future. It was imperative they be returned to their rightful owner. The man's expression when he saw the mare and colt would go a long way in convincing Dallas.

She was also looking forward to seeing Conner. They'd found a chance to be together at least a few hours every day since the charity event last Saturday. Each moment had been a whirlwind of excitement. She didn't know where things would ultimately lead, and tried not to dwell on it. Eventually, they'd have some decisions to make. Like when and what to tell Richard.

If he chose to, he could make things difficult for her and Conner. He already suspected something. He'd called just this morning for no reason in particular, and then again a few hours later. When she questioned him, he said he was concerned. That there was a difference in her voice.

A difference?

If Richard had noticed one small change in her, were others noticing, too?

She and Conner probably wouldn't be able to hide their relationship for much longer. That was fine with Dallas. When they were both ready, she was going to shout it to the world.

For now, she chose to concentrate on his job. The interview at Sonoran on Tuesday had gone well. Very well. While Sunday hadn't formally extended the offer—something about passing it by the board first—she'd inferred he had the job.

He had to be going crazy waiting to hear. Dallas was on pins and needles, jumping every time he called or texted. Maybe he'd get word this afternoon, and she'd be lucky enough to be with him. Then they'd *really* celebrate.

One less hurdle for them to overcome.

She still couldn't believe how accepting Conner was of the baby. Perhaps by the time she gave birth, they'd have such strong feelings for each other, be so secure in their relationship, that Richard's presence in their lives wouldn't make a difference.

The white SUV Dallas had been following for over a mile turned in to the drive leading to Powell Ranch. She slowed, and when they reached the office, parked alongside it.

Grabbing her camera bag, she bailed out of her car, and came to a stop. A young woman was assisting an elderly man from the SUV, situating his walker in front of him so that he could support himself as he stood. Dallas placed him in his late eighties, if not early nineties.

This had to be the owner of the mare. Supposed owner, she reminded herself. The photos and registration papers would determine that for sure.

She went up to them and smiled, something inside her softening. The pair didn't strike her as horse thieves or media thrill seekers, and there had been a few of those since the story broke.

"Hi, I'm Dallas. I work with the Powells. Are you by chance here about the mare and colt?"

"We are," the woman answered brightly, helping the man maneuver his walker over the uneven ground. "I'm Marjorie. This is my grandfather, Darius Edenvane."

"Welcome to Powell Ranch." She fell into step with them. "If Gavin's not in the office, you can wait there while I find him."

"I want to see my horse," the man said, his gravelly voice firm.

"Grandpa, shouldn't we meet with Mr. Powell first?"

He shook the walker, which had become stuck on a rock. "I can meet him in the barn just as easily."

"I'm sorry," Marjorie said. "When Grandpa makes up his mind, there's no changing it."

"No problem." Dallas pulled her phone from her pocket. "I'll have Gavin meet us at the mare's stall."

"Thank you, young lady." He gave his granddaughter a smug look. "See? She doesn't think I'm being difficult."

Marjorie simply smiled.

Dallas guessed the two had frequent arguments of a similar nature.

As they walked, she spoke to Gavin, who informed her that he and Conner would be right there. Her heart gave a small start at the mention of Conner. It had been only this morning since she'd seen him, and yet she couldn't wait.

Gavin and Conner were standing at the mare's stall when they arrived. Dallas made introductions, her gaze continually going to Conner. His smile lingered on her in return.

The elderly man and his granddaughter were oblivious, their attention elsewhere.

"Look, Grandpa. It's her," Marjorie said, her plain face made pretty by delight and amazement.

"I have eyes in my head. I can see it's her." Despite his grumpy protest, he was visibly moved.

The mare stuck her head over the stall door and sniffed at the man. First his sleeve, then his head. Snorting happily, she bumped him with her nose.

"Chiquita," he muttered affectionately, and stroked her face with his gnarled hand. "That's a good girl."

"We found her. I can't believe it." His granddaughter wiped her damp eyes. "We looked for months. Hated giving up but we had no choice. We just kept hoping she'd come home."

"How long has that been, Mr. Edenvane?" Gavin asked.

"Two years this January."

The timing coincided with what the vet had said about the length of time Chiquita had likely been roaming in the wild.

Distracted by the scene unfolding in front of her, Dallas almost forgot her camera. She hastily removed it from the bag and shot picture after picture, the most charming of which was the mare resting her large head on the man's shoulder. If he hadn't been grasping the walker, the weight would have toppled him.

Her own misty eyes made seeing through the viewfinder difficult.

"What a fine baby you have," he said. "Come here, little fellow."

The colt had edged closer, curious about the new visitors.

When the elderly man tried to pet him, he instantly darted behind his mother. After a moment, he inched forward once more, nostrils quivering. When the elderly man tried to pet him again, he allowed a single brief touch.

Dallas was shocked. Up till now, the only person who'd gotten close to the colt was Conner, who'd been working with him daily.

"If you want, we can trailer the horses to your place." Apparently Gavin didn't need to see any proof, either.

"Nothing I'd like better." Mr. Edenvane gave both horses another fond pat. "But my ranch got to be more'n I could handle, even with my granddaughter and her family living with me. I sold it off a year ago."

"We'd be happy to keep her here until you find a new home for her or sell her."

Sell her? Dallas was prepared for the mare and colt to go to their rightful owner, or even a friend of the owner. But sold? To strangers?

"Don't suppose you have any interest in buying her?" the elderly man asked. "Seeing as she's from some of the same original stock as your horses."

"She is?"

She was?

"Her lines go back sixty years. To the original mustangs that roamed this valley. We read up on you and your ranch before we came. On the internet. I know nothing about computers and have no intention of learning at my age. But Marjorie here's a whiz."

"You do a lot of great work for wild mustangs," she said, her gaze encompassing everyone. "I don't think Chiquita and her son could have a better home."

Please, please say yes!

"Sir, I'd very much like to own Chiquita. I'll pay you a fair price for her."

"The money's not important. But I do have a condition. I'd have to be able to come visit her whenever I had a hankering."

They shook hands. "You're welcome anytime."

Dallas held back the tears. She felt Conner's touch on her arm and shrugged, as if to make light of her weepy display. He winked, letting her know she wasn't fooling him.

"We brought her papers," Mr. Edenvane said.

"Why don't we go inside? Have a cold drink."

"Don't suppose you have something a bit stiffer? Marjorie's always hiding my Jack Daniels."

"Oh, Grandpa. I only hide it because of the kids."

He harrumphed.

Gavin chuckled. "No Jack Daniels, but I might have a bottle of Jim Beam tucked away."

"I think you and I can be friends."

"I'm counting on it."

"Before we go in, I'd like to see that mustang stallion of yours. If you don't mind."

"Don't mind at all."

Mr. Edenvane ran his gnarled hand along Chiquita's neck one last time, pausing at the healing wound. "They ever find the son of a bitch who did this to her, I swear I'll wring his neck."

"I'll be in line right behind you," Gavin said.

They started down the barn aisle.

"It's a ways to Prince's stall."

"I can make it."

When no one was paying attention, Conner brushed Dallas's fingers. She would have liked to take his arm, but they weren't ready for public displays of affection.

Telling Gavin, Ethan and Clay was another of those hurdles looming in the distance.

Frankly, she wasn't completely confident of their response. They'd probably be happy for their friend. They did like Dallas, after all. But they might worry about Conner taking on too much by dating a woman carrying another man's baby.

They wouldn't be out of line, either. Dallas imagined all their family and friends would feel the same.

"I could be wrong, but I think that colt is out of your stallion." Mr. Edenvane sat on the living room couch next to his granddaughter. He sipped a whiskey while she drank iced tea.

"We'll know soon." Dallas had told them about the DNA testing on the colt after Mr. Edenvane had seen Prince and remarked on their resemblance.

To her, the colt looked like his mother. Mr. Edenvane saw things she didn't. The shape of the colt's head. His body structure. His temperament.

"The vet's expecting the results any day," she continued.

"Will you call me when you hear?"

"Absolutely," Gavin assured him.

He stood next to the wingback chair where Sage sat holding Milo. The baby sucked his thumb and stared at the twirling ceiling fan, disinterested in anything or anyone else. Dallas and Conner were squeezed together on the love seat. Another time, she might have been acutely aware of his nearness. Today, Mr. Edenvane had her full attention.

She couldn't say why she found him so fascinating. Despite his withered and frail body, his eyes were bright and intelligent and his wit sharp as a tack. She'd love to take his picture in a different setting other than the barn. His granddaughter, too. The way she gazed at him with respect and devotion… there was a story there.

"Tell us about Chiquita," Conner prompted. "Where did you get her?"

"Had her parents. Grandparents and great-grandparents, too. They came with the ranch when I bought it."

"You aren't from here?"

"West Virginia born and raised. Moved my wife and boys out here in the mid-fifties, I guess it was. When I bought that place, there wasn't so much as another shack for twenty miles."

Mr. Edenvane's ranch was on the east side of the McDowell Mountains, near the Verde River. Chiquita had traveled far in her wanderings.

He took another sip of his drink. "I was told by the man I bought the place from that he traded with the Pimas for the horses. In those days, mustangs were still roaming all over these parts. About the time I bought the ranch is when they disappeared for good. Or so the stories go."

Something in his tone made Dallas curious. "You believe differently."

"I saw them. Horses. Plenty of times."

Dallas scooted to the edge of her seat cushion. "Tell us about it."

"In the mountains. Along the river. On the reservation. Always a small herd, six or eight head. They'd come to my ranch when water was scarce and vegetation lean. After they busted down my fences enough times, I started putting hay out for them. Be gone the next morning, every last stalk. They disappeared about ten years ago."

"Only ten years ago?" She turned to Conner. Prince wasn't much younger than that.

"Bud Duvall has a story like yours," he said.

"I know him. A cattle rancher. His son owns that rodeo arena."

"Bud and his father rescued a small herd when he was just a boy," Conner continued. "They kept the horses, incorporated them in their breeding stock. That had to be…forty years ago."

"Lots of ranchers did back then."

"But you saw horses more recently."

"Don't know where they went. I guess too many houses being built for their tastes. Except for your stallion." He nodded at Gavin. "I'm willing to bet he's from that herd. The last one."

The room went utterly quiet.

Gavin rubbed a knuckle along his jaw. "There's no way to know for certain."

"Have Prince DNA tested." Everyone looked at Dallas. "There are plenty of horses here on Powell Ranch related to the original wild mustangs."

"How much can the DNA test tell?"

"Ask Dr. Schaeffer."

"Can you call him?" Sage suggested. "It would be nice to find out while Mr. Edenvane and Marjorie are still here."

Gavin took out his phone and placed the call. While he waited to be put through to the vet, everyone chatted softly. Dallas smiled hopefully at Conner, who squeezed her knee.

"If none of the horses here are a match," he said, "we might try some of Clay's. He has a few older head that his father owned."

"Dr. Schaeffer, thank you for taking my call." Gavin explained the situation to the vet. They spoke for several minutes, Dallas hanging on every word. "Yeah, we could probably take the samples, save you a trip out here. Sure thing. I'll hold." He covered the mouthpiece. "He's checking with the girl at the front desk to see if the lab has sent the colt's DNA results yet."

Sage stood. "I'm going to put Milo down for a nap. Can I get anyone a refill on their drink or a snack?"

Everyone was fine. In Dallas's case, she was too nervous to even think about eating. Conner must have stopped caring about keeping their relationship under wraps, for he took her hand firmly in his.

It felt nice. Right. The way it should be.

"Yeah, Doc." Gavin straightened. "I'm here." His broad grin conveyed the good news that the test results were positive. "Thanks for your help. See you on Friday."

He hung up, and the room erupted in laughter and hugs.

"Chiquita's colt really is Prince's son." Dallas couldn't get over it.

"I figured as much the moment I laid eyes on your stallion." For a split second, Mr. Edenvane's face was that of a young man.

Dallas longed for her camera.

"Grandpa never got over losing Chiquita," Marjorie said. "I'm so happy with the way things turned out."

Mr. Edenvane raised his glass as if to toast. "She's a fine one. You'll enjoy riding her once she's healed. Has the smoothest gait of any horse I owned. Like riding a bike."

"This is going to make an incredible new ending for the book." Dallas jumped to her feet. "We need more pictures. Mr. Edenvane, would you and Marjorie be willing to pose for me?"

The elderly man was pleased to oblige and, Dallas thought, flattered. She promised to send him and his granddaughter sets of the pictures. Gavin promised them each copies of the book when it was published.

The mood was exuberant after that. It had taken a year, but Prince's origin was close to being determined.

Conner watched while Dallas took Mr. Edenvane's photograph on the back patio. She realized there would be no more working with him after today.

She was a little sad to see the project wrapping up. She consoled herself with the knowledge that every time she looked at the book it would be a reminder of these last wonderful weeks and the events that had brought her and Conner together.

"You going to tell me what's going on with you and Dallas?"

Conner looked Gavin directly in the face, and then turned away. He might as well be wearing a sign on his forehead. "We're friends."

"Like you and I are friends?"

"Sort of."

"Except we don't hold hands."

"All right. It's a little more than friendship."

"A little? Ha! From where I stand, you're in deep. Up to your elbows, if not your neck.

It was true.

"We had a date."

"And?"

"And then another date. Dinner."

"Did there happen to be breakfast in bed following the dinner?"

Conner refused to discuss the intimate aspects of his relationship with Dallas, even with Gavin.

The two of them were standing on the back porch. Mr. Edenvane and his granddaughter had recently left. Dallas was inside the house, playing with Milo while Sage readied the girls for a choral concert at school that evening. Gavin had lured Conner outside under the pretense of talking ranch business.

"What about her ex? Your old buddy? Does he know?"

"Not yet."

"That's going to be interesting."

"Yeah."

"Have you even thought about telling him?"

"I try not to." Right or wrong, Conner was choosing to live in the moment. It was easier that way. The last six months had been the worst in his life, next to when his parents divorced. He deserved a few days, a few weeks, of happiness. "We're not making any announcements yet. And I'd appreciate it if you didn't say anything."

"You don't want people to know, you'd better keep your hands to yourself."

Good advice.

"What changed your mind?" Gavin leaned against the patio

wall and folded his arms over his chest. "Last you told me, you weren't going to ask her out."

"The Sonoran Bottling Plant board meeting is scheduled for tomorrow morning." Conner hadn't mentioned it to Dallas, in order not to worry her. "I should hear back in the afternoon."

"After you land the job, what then?"

"Dallas and I will talk. Get an understanding of each other's expectations."

"Better hurry. She's a woman, she's already forming expectations."

"I will." Conner pushed his cowboy hat back and rubbed his forehead.

When Gavin next spoke, his voice was less stern. "You have nothing to be scared of."

"Wouldn't you be in my shoes?"

"Hell, yes. But not because I didn't have the kind of job I wanted. Great as Dallas is, she comes with a lot of built-in complications. Those are what would scare me."

"Hear that sound? It's my knees knocking together."

Sage stuck her head out the door. "Dallas is leaving. Come say goodbye."

Gavin pushed off the wall. "You need anything, a shoulder to cry on, a swift kick in the ass, let me know."

"Thanks." Conner managed a dry chuckle.

In the kitchen, Dallas was loading her camera bag and purse. "Hey!" She broke into a smile at the sight of him.

Seeing Sage's raised eyebrows, Conner figured Gavin wasn't the only one who'd figured out which way the wind was blowing.

"I tried to get her to stay for dinner, but she refuses," Sage said.

"I have to pick up some prints and deliver them before five." Dallas jammed more papers in her bag. "This is one of those clients you don't show up late for."

That gave her an hour, if she didn't dally.

With no more reason to keep secrets, Conner said, "I'll walk you to your car."

"Okay." She smiled again, the familiar, I-can't-wait-to-be-alone-with-you kind.

Conner's gut knotted. He really should have that talk with her soon. Tomorrow. After he got the formal job offer from Sonoran Bottling. When he felt strong and confident and like his old self.

They had just reached her car when her phone rang. Fishing it from the depths of her purse, she checked the display and answered, a puzzled expression on her face.

Was it Richard? The guy had made a habit of calling Dallas a lot lately.

"Yes, this Dallas Sorrenson. How can I help you?"

Okay, not Richard.

"I did. I can. Absolutely, I will." There were pauses in between each of her remarks. "Tomorrow at 11:00 a.m. No, no, I can look up the address. Oh, all right. It's Dallas Sorrenson at Cox dot net. Great. Thank you so much for this opportunity! Uh-huh. See you then."

She snapped her cell phone shut, her face aglow. "That was Channel Three. They want to interview me for their noon edition of the *Arizona Today* show." She threw her arms around Conner and squeezed tightly.

"About Chiquita?"

"Yes. Also about my volunteer work at the animal shelters and the mustang sanctuary. Apparently, when they heard Chiquita's story, they researched me. Channel Three researched me!" She squealed. "This is an incredible break. For the shelters, the ranch and for me."

"You deserve it." He drew her to him for a quick kiss on the lips. "You've worked hard. For a long time. Your photographs are the kind that inspire people."

"It's really not that big of a deal. The entire world doesn't watch the noon edition of *Arizona Today*."

"Don't sell yourself or this opportunity short." He tilted her face to his. "Who knows what will happen? You could become the next great documentary photographer. Another Dorothea Lange."

"True." The glow returned, coloring her cheeks an appealing shade of pink.

"What me to go with you?"

"You'd do that?"

"Sure. Gavin will give me the time off."

"I'd love for you to come with me."

"I'll pick you up at ten."

He waited for her to suggest he meet her later that evening at her place and spend the night.

She didn't.

"Great. Oh, gosh! I really need to get going. I can't be late delivering those prints."

Another quick kiss and she was gone, heading down the driveway to the road as if running a race.

Conner didn't return to Gavin's house or his apartment. Rather, he walked to the barn and straight to Chiquita's stall. He liked that she had a name at last, and called her by it.

When he didn't produce a treat, she ignored him. The colt, however, came over. Conner had been working with him every day, trying to get him used to people. As if sensing his mood, the colt rested his chin on Conner's arm.

In his mind, he saw Dallas driving away. She wasn't just heading to an appointment, she was heading to her bright, shining future. Ready to make her mark on the world.

He only hoped she wasn't leaving him behind.

Chapter Fourteen

"Wow!" Conner gave a low whistle. "You look fantastic!"

"Not too pregnant?" Dallas stepped out onto the stoop, closing and locking her front door behind her.

"No one will notice."

They would be too busy staring at her legs, which were showed off to their best advantage in a slim fitting skirt. The loose blazer she'd chosen to wear over the skirt mostly camouflaged her condition.

Personally, Conner liked her slightly protruding belly and thought it made her sexier.

"Thank you, sweetie." Standing on tiptoes, she kissed his cheek and wiped off the lipstick smudge she'd left behind. "Sorry about that."

He had half a mind to pull her into his arms and let her leave lipstick smudges all over his mouth. He waited too long. The next instant she was off, walking briskly toward the curb, where his truck was parked. He should have thought ahead and asked Clay to lend him his car again. Maybe Dallas didn't want to ride to the TV station in his jalopy.

"I have some news," she said when they were on their way. "The AAWA called after I got home yesterday. They want to use my pictures of Chiquita for their anticruelty campaign. Website, posters, magazines and newspapers. If the campaign's successful, the ads could be picked up nationally."

"Congratulations!"

"I'm glad some good has come out of that poor horse's ordeal. Maybe the next person will think twice before abusing an animal. Or maybe someone will have the guts to come forward and report the abuses."

To date, the authorities had no idea who had shot Chiquita or why, and they probably never would.

"There's more," she said, her eyes twinkling.

"What?"

Conner was happy to let her talk. It kept him from dwelling on the Sonoran Bottling board meeting that was probably taking place that very moment.

"I sold the picture of you and Molly. The one I took when we went on the wagon ride."

"You're kidding."

"Found out right before you arrived." She flipped the visor down to block the sun as they turned a corner. "Creative Marketing Associates bought it. They're huge! And get this. One of their clients is Sonoran Bottling. What are the odds?"

Conner's anticipation escalated. "Did *they* buy the photograph?"

"No, but wouldn't that have been cool? An auto dealership did, that's all I know."

"Still, it's good, right?"

"It's great. People from all over the state are going to see my work. And your face." She grinned gleefully.

His face in a magazine? Hard to imagine.

"The pay is good." She cited the amount he'd receive for the model's fee.

"That's a lot. I didn't do anything except stand there."

"You got lucky. We both did. A photographer never knows which of their pictures will sell and for how much."

"I'm not sure I feel right about taking the money. You're the one who did all the work."

"I wouldn't have had a picture without you." She laughed. "Maybe we should try again. Then we'll both make a bundle and become famous."

"That'd be the day," he said drily.

"It could happen."

Conner should be pleased. He certainly needed the money. If only it didn't come from Dallas.

"Hey, you."

He glanced over to find her watching him.

"Anything wrong?" she asked.

She was floating on air. He didn't want to do or say anything to spoil her mood.

"Just wondering what a TV set is like."

"It's not what you think. I went a few times with my mom when I was a kid. Sometimes she'd be a guest on one of the PBS shows. Usually having to do with the school or sculpting or an art showing."

"Were you ever on TV?"

"No, and I'm a little nervous." For the next few minutes, Dallas regaled him with stories of her mother's experiences. Then her phone rang. "It's Richard," she announced, glaring at the display.

Conner tried to act as if he wasn't listening to their conversation, which he was.

"I did. Thanks for stopping by."

Stopping by? He'd been over to see her?

"No, I'll definitely use it."

Use what? Something for the baby? For her?

"I've been thinking. Haven't decided yet."

Thinking about what?

Conner wanted to but couldn't shut off the questions, which kept coming one after the other.

"Can we talk later? This isn't a good time." She finally

rolled her eyes, communicating her impatience and that she wished the phone call was over.

Was it true or strictly for Conner's benefit?

"We're on our way to the TV station. For the interview. I told you last night."

So they had talked last night. In person, apparently, because Richard had dropped something off. Was that why Dallas hadn't invited Conner to stay over?

This had to stop. Now.

He forced his attention fully on the road. Traffic was increasing the closer they traveled to downtown Phoenix. Dallas had every right and reason to talk to Richard, the father of her baby, and would be doing so the rest of their lives. Conner had better get used to it.

"A friend, is all. Someone I work with."

What would Richard say if he knew the friend was Conner? Probably be as jealous as Conner was of him.

"I have to go," Dallas said brusquely. "Yes. I will. Call you later." Expelling a tired sigh, she leaned her head against the rest. "I really didn't want that right before the interview."

Conner contemplated putting a reassuring hand on her knee, but didn't.

"There's nothing between Richard and me," she said.

"What?"

"In case you're wondering."

"I wasn't."

"You're grinding your teeth."

He immediately stopped. "Traffic's congested. I'm suppressing road rage."

She reached over, pried one of his hands loose from the steering wheel and held it in hers. "Look at me, Conner."

He did. For two seconds, because traffic really was congested.

She squeezed his fingers until he relaxed.

They stayed like that, holding hands, until a phone chimed. This time it was his.

Sonoran Bottling came up on the display, and a lightning streak of exhilaration cut through him.

"I think it's Sunday Givens."

"Pull over," Dallas instructed.

Placing the phone to his ear, he swung the truck into the first entrance they came to, which happened to be a bank. "Hello. This is Conner Durham."

Dallas shut off the radio.

"Conner, hi. It's Sunday Givens. How are you today?"

"I'm fine. Nice to hear from you."

"Is this a good time to talk?"

He pulled into an empty space and parked, letting the engine idle. "I have a few minutes."

"I can't tell you what a good fit you are for the position and what a delight it's been, getting to know you. The board was very impressed by you and your résumé, and they're not easily swayed. There isn't one candidate I've interviewed I like better than you."

"Thank you."

Here it came. She was going to extend the official offer! Beside him, Dallas beamed.

"Which is why," Sunday continued, "it's so difficult for me to deliver this news."

Inch by inch, Conner's vision dimmed until only the center of the steering wheel remained.

"I'm sorry. The board chose another candidate. One whose experience is more closely aligned with a bottling plant than energy systems are. I could overrule their decision, but I don't feel it's warranted under the circumstances."

He was quite sure his heart had stopped beating. That something inside him had broken.

"Conner? Did I lose you?" Sunday's voice sounded a hundred miles away.

"I understand." His tone was flat. Empty.

"If this individual turns out not be the best choice, we'll absolutely bring you on board."

The rest of what she said was an unintelligible humming. He hadn't gotten the job. They'd hired someone else.

Evidently he must have muttered a response, for Sunday apologized again, wished him well and bade him goodbye.

"Oh, Conner." Dallas leaned across the console and stroked his arm. "I'm sorry. I know how much you wanted that job."

He had, and his disappointment at not landing it left a giant, gaping hole inside him. Three days wasted when he could have been job hunting. What if the ideal one had been posted and he missed it?

Anger rose up in him like an exploding geyser.

Swearing, he threw the truck in Reverse and peeled out of the parking lot, slowing only when he reached the road. He had a passenger, a pregnant passenger. Now wasn't the time to vent his frustration by driving recklessly.

He and Dallas spoke little on the remaining drive to the TV station. Conner reminded himself over and over that it could be worse. He still had employment, even if he didn't earn enough to cover all his expenses. If he swallowed his pride, sold the house at a substantial loss, he'd be better off.

If he could even sell it. The real estate market wasn't what it used to be.

Dammit! That would teach him to assume.

At the TV station, he held open the glass door at the front entrance for Dallas, attempting to quell the tremors in his arms and legs.

She went ahead to the front desk and checked in. They were escorted by a very pregnant assistant something-or-other down a series of winding halls to a studio.

Conner didn't generally watch the *Arizona Today* show, but he'd caught bits of it now and then and he recognized the set. Dallas was correct when she'd said it would look different than on TV.

"Please wait here." The woman pointed to a director's chair positioned a considerable distance off set. "Ms. Sorrenson, if you'll come with me."

"Where are we going?"

"Hair and makeup."

Dallas's fingers flew to her hair and then her cheek.

"Just a touch-up. For the lights." The woman gave her a once-over. "You look fine. And congratulations. When are you due?"

"Early April."

"Your first?"

"Yes.

The woman patted her large belly in a manner similar to how Dallas patted her smaller one. "My second." She turned to Conner. "You must be excited, Dad. There's nothing like having your first baby."

Conner waited for Dallas to correct the woman, tell her that he wasn't the baby's father.

Instead she stammered something about her parents and this being their first grandchild.

He tried not to read too much into it as he watched the two of them walk away. Dallas was nervous. Distracted. She might not even have noticed the other woman's comment.

He observed the camera operators, stage manager, director and an array of other workers scurrying to and fro, half of them wearing headsets. It was an interesting process and completely unfamiliar to Conner. He'd have taken more of an interest if he wasn't replaying the phone call with Sunday over and over in his head.

Eventually, two cohosts emerged, took their places in the

stylish, ultramodern chairs, and the show began. Conner barely followed what was said, their supercharged personalities annoying him. A commercial break was followed by more of the show and another commercial break. When they returned, Dallas was introduced.

She entered the set, looking stunning. Conner concentrated, listened to her answer with poise and confidence the questions put to her. A nearby TV monitor showed what the viewers at home were seeing.

After a warning from the hosts about viewer discretion, photos of Chiquita appeared, the arrows protruding. Then close-ups of her ghastly wounds. The hosts expressed appropriate outrage and sympathy. The interview continued briefly before taking a surprising turn. Dallas's other accomplishments were mentioned and praised, several of her commercial photographs shown. She accepted the compliments humbly and with grace.

Her career would skyrocket after today. How could it not? And she deserved everything coming to her.

Didn't Conner deserve more than he had? Hadn't he worked just as hard as Dallas? Just as hard as Richard? He possessed two degrees. Had given years of loyal, dedicated, exemplary service to his employer.

He blinked, realizing Dallas's interview was over and he'd missed the end. When had she left the set?

She must be waiting in the green room or whatever they called it.

The assistant something-or-other appeared in front of him. "Did you like the show, Mr. Sorrenson?"

"Uh, yeah."

"Your wife's a natural."

Say it. Tell her Dallas isn't your wife.

"What do you do for a living?"

"A…ranch."

The woman looked impressed. "You own a ranch?"

"Work on one."

"Oh." She was no longer impressed.

It didn't matter that he'd once earned three times what she probably did, had owned a garage full of vehicles and vacationed every year in exciting locales.

He was nothing but a ranch hand who deserved no more than an "Oh."

How soon until Dallas said it with that exact same telltale tone?

People on their way up in the world didn't usually remain long with someone on his way down.

"Are you all right, Mr. Sorrenson?" The woman leaned closer. "Can I get you some water?"

"Air."

"I'm sorry?"

"I need air." His lungs seemed to have filled with a dense fiber that blocked the flow of oxygen. "And my name is Durham. Conner Durham. Not Sorrenson."

He stood and stumbled past the woman, instinctively heading though the maze of hallways to the front entrance. Only when he was outside could he draw a decent breath.

"THANKS, MOM." Dallas cradled her cell phone between her shoulder and ear. "I'll be by later."

"For dinner?"

She smiled. "Sure. We can watch the show together."

For the second time, Dallas thought. She'd set her own DVR to record the *Arizona Today* show and planned on watching the episode the minute she arrived home. Hopefully, with Conner, if he didn't have to leave immediately for work.

Work at the ranch, not the bottling plant. She still didn't quite know what to say to him. He'd rebuffed all her efforts.

"See you around six," Marina said. "And bring Conner."

"All right. We'll see. Love you, Mom." Studying his stoic expression, Dallas gave another stab at starting a conversation with him. "She said the interview went really well."

"It did."

Finally, he spoke! They were almost at her house and hadn't exchanged four words since she'd found him waiting outside the TV station.

"I didn't come off too silly? I wasn't expecting them to show any photos other than the ones of Chiquita."

"That woman, the pregnant one, she called you a natural."

"Really?" Pleasure and pride flowed through Dallas. She'd wanted to do well. The call from Richard and then Conner's bad news had thrown her off balance. She was glad that hadn't come across.

"I'm sure you'll get a lot of new clients after today."

"You think?" She checked her cell phone. No text message or voice mail icons were flashing.

Well, that was stupid. As if a call would come in so soon after the show.

"What's most important is that we find the person who shot Chiquita and prevent something like that from ever happening again. It's why I did the interview, not to generate new business."

Though it would be nice.

"There's nothing wrong with accomplishing both."

He'd waited such a long time before responding, she'd begun to think he'd retreated behind that wall again.

"Mom invited us to dinner tonight. You and me. To watch the show with them. She recorded it."

There was another pause before he answered. "I'm working late. To make up for taking off this morning."

Dallas didn't quite believe him, but she let it slide. He was wounded. Parading her good fortune in front of him made it worse. She'd give him whatever time he needed to recover, including distance from her for an evening if that was what he wanted.

It wasn't what she wanted, however. If she could, she'd wrap him in her arms and hold him until his pain lessened.

They reached her condo, and he parked where he usually did along the curb.

Usually? Had their relationship progressed to that point?

Yes. They were involved. Intimate. A couple.

But were they capable of handling the multitude of challenges facing them? The baby. Richard. Conner's financial worries and employment situation. Her recent successes.

She was capable. She was less certain of Conner.

Before this morning, before the phone call from Sunday Givens, she'd have counted on him without a single hesitation. Now, he'd withdrawn. Shut her out instead of accepting the support she willingly tendered.

That wasn't what couples did.

It was temporary, Dallas told herself. He'd take a few well-deserved hours to brood and then he'd be back to his old self.

If only he'd gotten the job. How different the ride home would have been.

He walked her to her door.

She dug for her keys. "Want to come in?"

"I have to..."

"Work. I know." She circled his neck with her free arm, intending to kiss him.

To her surprise, he set her aside. "I've changed my mind. I will come in for a few minutes."

"Good." Except the look in his eyes was anything but good. Something serious, something more than the job, was eating at him.

In the kitchen, she deposited her purse and portfolio on the table. Conner, she noticed, didn't remove his hat or jacket.

Charming and Snow White both appeared, but remained under the kitchen table, watching with wide, owl-like eyes.

"I have an idea," Dallas announced, infusing her voice with cheerfulness. "Let me call the head of the AAWA."

"About Chiquita?"

"No, you. The association is large, and even though they're nonprofit, they have all kinds of paid positions. Several at the management level."

He spoke slowly. "For me?"

"Yes, for you." She went to him, slid her arms into his jacket and around his waist. "I could also contact a few of my clients. Ask if they're hiring."

"No." He stiffened.

"It can't hurt to ask."

He pulled away from her so fast she was left standing alone in the middle of the floor.

"I don't need your handouts. I can find a job on my own."

"It's not a handout. I'm just trying to help."

"I get it. You'd rather have a boyfriend with a real job. A good job. One you can brag about to your friends. Like Richard. Not someone who's just a ranch hand."

She gasped sharply. "That isn't true."

"Isn't it?" Conner's features were a storm of hurt and anger. "What do you say when your friends ask you what I do for a living?"

"I say you're a systems analyst. Which you are. And while you're looking for a new job, you're running the mustang sanctuary, managing the livestock at Clay's rodeo arena and in charge of training horses at Powell Ranch."

"I'm none of those things."

"Yes, you are."

"I work for Gavin. Just like I work for Clay. I'm not running or managing or in charge of anything. And I'm an out-of-work systems analyst. You make me sound better than I am."

"You are better. I don't have to—"

"That woman at the TV station called me Mr. Sorrenson."

Was that what was bothering him?

"It's a natural mistake. People called me Mrs. Kassor all the time when Richard and I were engaged."

"She also assumed I was your baby's father. Why didn't you set her straight?"

Why hadn't she?

She shrugged. "I didn't think about it. I was concentrating on the interview."

Okay, he was upset about the Sonoran Bottling job going to someone else. But Dallas had done nothing wrong. She'd shown compassion and sympathy. Had tried to console and encourage him. So she painted him in the best possible way to her friends. Who wasn't guilty of that?

"Whatever I did to upset you, Conner, tell me. Please."

"I am what I am. Making me sound better doesn't change me."

"I'm not trying to change you. I don't care what you do for a living as long as you're happy."

"That's just it. I'm not happy. I don't want to be a ranch hand forever. But I'm not ashamed of it, either."

"Neither am I. I'm proud of what you do."

"Then why don't you tell people the truth?"

"What's wrong with casting things in the best possible light?"

"That power of positive thinking you're always pushing?"

She'd mind less if his tone wasn't snide. "It's not my fault my career is taking off and you still haven't found a job," she stated.

He recoiled.

"I'm sorry, Conner. That was thoughtless." And much crueler than what he'd said to her.

"I should go."

Panic seized her. "Wait!" She reached for him.

"What if I never find a job? What if I lose my house and deplete my 401K? You really want to be tied to a penniless loser?"

"You're not a loser! That's your disappointment talking."

"Damn right I'm disappointed. I'm good at what I do. Very good. I'd have run circles around Sonoran's last systems analyst. Except they didn't give me the chance."

"Their mistake. But someone else will hire you."

"When?" He shook his head. "You're having a baby, Dallas. You need a man who can bring more to the relationship that I can. One who's secure. Responsible. Not a liability."

Was he referring to Richard?

"You're wonderful with children."

"That's hardly enough."

"It is for me. And you—" She started to say "love me" and thought better of it. "You care for me."

"I can't alter how I feel. How I was raised. I have to be on a more equal career and financial footing with the woman in my life. I don't begrudge you your success. You deserve it. But watching you is hard on me."

"This is temporary. You'll find a job."

"I will. Eventually. It could take a while, though. Months. Years."

"And we'll keep doing what we're doing in the meantime."

Another one of those long pauses followed. Dallas sensed what was coming before he said it.

"I think we should take a break."

Tears pricked her eyes. "You mean *break up?*"

"It might be for the best."

"No! No, no, no. Let's just take a minute here and calm down. Think about things."

"There's nothing to think about. Your baby and your career are your priorities. Mine are finding a job and not losing my house."

Her patience snapped. "All this because some woman at the TV station called you Mr. Sorrenson by mistake?"

"It was the shot in the arm I needed to see this—us— clearer."

"I won't give up opportunities simply because you've hit a bump in the road."

"I wouldn't expect you to."

Her cell phone rang. She ignored it.

"Tell me, and be honest. If the situation was reversed, if I was the one out of work and you had a job, would we still be having this conversation?"

He didn't answer.

"Yeah, that's what I thought." She wiped her damp eyes. "You're a male chauvinist, Conner."

"Maybe a little."

"A little? You're about to walk out on the best thing to ever happen to you because you don't have as good a job as I do."

He wasn't the only one guilty of having an inflated ego.

"If I'm not satisfied with the state of my life, how can you ever be satisfied with it?"

At that moment, her land line rang. She ignored it as she had her cell phone.

"Take care, Dallas. Give your parents my apologies for missing dinner."

What? He was walking out on her and all he could say was to apologize to her parents?

The answering machine on the counter picked up and the greeting played. They both turned their heads when Richard's voice filled the air.

"Hey, honey. I went home at lunch and watched your interview. You knocked 'em dead. And your pictures…wow. Call me later, okay? I'd like to come over. Talk to you." His voice went soft near the end.

The best camera shot in the world couldn't have fully captured the misery on Conner's face.

"It's not what you think," she insisted.

"You have no idea what I'm thinking."

And she wasn't sure she wanted to know.

He left then. She didn't see him to the door. Her legs would only carry her as far as the table, where she slumped into a chair.

Her land line rang again. Another message, this one from the ad agency.

"Dallas! Call the minute you get this. We've had three clients express an interest in your work. All in the last hour. That TV interview must have been phenomenal. You rock, girl!"

She should be thrilled. This was exactly the response she'd been hoping for.

Only without Conner to share it with, she didn't care.

Chapter Fifteen

"Quit your fussing." Conner stroked the colt's neck, and felt him tremble beneath his fingers. "You're not hurt."

It had taken a dozen attempts, but he now had a pony-size halter on the colt. Of course, he hated it. When they were done, he'd jerked away from Conner and pranced in circles around the pen before coming to stand next to his mother.

Chiquita wasn't interested in the least, and her calm demeanor helped relax her offspring. Neither had she objected earlier when Conner attached the lunge line and put her through her paces for a good half hour.

Her injuries weren't healed nearly enough for a saddle to be placed on her back. That would require another month or two. In the meantime, Conner would exercise her regularly with a lunge line in the round pen.

Almost two years living in the wild hadn't affected her much. She was intelligent, responsive and eager to please. Conner had no doubt old Mr. Edenvane was right. The mare would make a fine trail horse. She was already an excellent and proven broodmare.

The colt? Well, the jury was still out on him. He'd been born wild and would require a lot of training.

In the young horse's favor, Conner would have plenty of time to invest in him. Conner had no day job other than being a ranch hand, and no girlfriend to occupy his evenings and weekends.

If he concentrated really hard on the horses, he could forget about Dallas and their breakup. For a minute. Two at the most.

He hadn't called her, and she hadn't called him. What did he expect? That she'd come running to Powell Ranch, begging him to take her back?

Hardly. Not after the awful things he'd said to her.

If anyone was owed an apology, it was her. And he would apologize. Soon. When he could face her again without feeling an invisible knife twisting in his gut.

Terrible, hurtful words aside, they were better off apart.

The colt bumped his arm and pawed the ground impatiently.

"You want some attention, huh?" Conner rubbed the colt's nose, which made him snort and shake his head. "Must mean you've decided the halter's not so bad."

"You name that colt yet?" Gavin stood at the railing, his boot resting on the bottom rung.

How long had he been standing there?

"Thought you were going to do that."

"Me? No. I don't name other people's horses."

Conner shielded his eyes and squinted at his friend. "Other people's horses? He's yours."

"No, he's yours. You found him. You captured him and the mare. You're the only one he'll let within ten feet of him. The way I see it, he belongs to you. He seems to think so, too."

Conner was deeply touched. He'd grown fond of the little guy. But he couldn't accept. "I can't afford a horse right now." If he didn't come up with another two hundred dollars by the end of the week, he'd be late making the mortgage payment on his house.

"He doesn't eat much. Consider it a bonus."

"I may not be able to afford him when he starts eating

more." Conner stared at the ground. God, he despised being broke.

"Name him," Gavin insisted.

"Why?"

"Once you do, he's really yours."

Conner did want the colt, but he couldn't take on another responsibility.

"You can work an extra couple hours a week to pay for his feed and board."

"I need every spare minute to look for a real job." He sent Gavin a remorseful glance. "No offense."

"None taken. You're a good cowboy and horses are a passion of yours. But they're not your calling. Not like the rest of us."

The rest of us being Gavin, Ethan and Clay.

Conner untied Chiquita's lead rope and led her out of the pen. The colt, still nameless, pranced at her side.

"What's really wrong?" Gavin asked, shutting the gate behind them.

"I didn't get the job with Sonoran Bottling. They called Wednesday."

"You're only just telling me now?"

"I don't know why I'm so bothered. It's hardly the first job I wanted and didn't get."

"You weren't dating Dallas then."

"I'm not dating her now."

"I realize you two haven't made any big announcement, but I'm pretty sure what you're doing is dating."

"We're not dating," he repeated.

Gavin looked confused. "Since when?"

"Wednesday."

"Same day you found out about the job at the bottling plant? Hmm. Fancy that."

"It wasn't going to work."

"Because you're not good enough for her."

As often as Conner had thought it the last few days, hearing someone say it—his friend no less—stung.

"Something you concluded all by yourself, and based solely on the bottling plant job tanking."

"She needs to decide once and for all if she's going to marry Richard." Conner began leading the horses toward the barn.

Gavin walked beside him. "She decided that a long time ago when she ended their engagement."

"You didn't hear the phone message he left her."

"You're making a bigger deal of this than it is."

"The reason he has hope for a reconciliation is because she hasn't cut him off completely."

"They're having a baby together. He's always going to be leaving her phone messages. Better they're on good terms than bad ones. I know. I go through this every day with Cassie and her mom, and Isa and her dad. There's nothing I'd like better than to strangle Sage's ex."

"There's a difference. Sage's ex doesn't want to marry her."

"You're right. And I'm not sure how I'd feel if he still loved her and was actively pursuing her."

"Not good. That's how you'd feel."

"Probably. But you can bet I wouldn't be using her ex-fiancé as an excuse."

"Meaning?

"The problem is you. Not Dallas and not Richard."

"He has a lot more going for him than I do."

"Except that she doesn't love him."

They reached Chiquita's stall. Conner led her in and removed her halter. He left the colt's halter on, and would for the next few weeks, until the little guy got used to it.

"She doesn't love me, either."

"That's about the biggest crock of horseshit I've heard in a long time," Gavin said. "She's crazy about you."

"If she is, she shouldn't be."

"What's gotten into you?" The growl in Gavin's voice took Conner aback. "Has your spine gone completely soft?"

Back in their younger days, when they were playing sports and rodeoing, those would have been fighting words.

Hell, they still were.

There, in the middle of the barn aisle, Conner grabbed a fistful of Gavin's jacket and hauled him up until their faces were just inches apart. "My spine's not soft."

A wide smile split Gavin's face. "There's the Conner Durham I know. It's good to have you back, buddy."

Conner's grip on Gavin's jacket loosened. Bit by bit, his own mouth stretched into a slow grin.

He felt better than he had in days. Months. Seven months, to be exact.

The office door swung open and Javier tumbled out into the aisle. He took one look at Conner and Gavin and hesitated, apparently deciding it was better not to interrupt.

"What is it, *amigo?*" Gavin asked.

"A man…he here."

Gavin stepped back from Conner and smoothed his jacket. "I'll be right along."

"No, *señor.* He come for Conner."

"Me?" Conner tugged his own jacket into place. "Did he tell you his name? *Qué es su nombre?*"

Javier completely mangled the pronunciation.

Even so, Conner recognized it, and his gut clenched.

What was Richard doing here, and what did he want with him?

THE SHARP KNOCKING on her front door gave Dallas a jolt. She wasn't expecting anyone, not at—she glanced at the clock on the stove—3:58 in the afternoon.

Please, she thought to herself as she padded across the living room to check the peephole, *don't let it be Conner.* She wasn't ready to see him yet.

Don't let it be Richard, either, she added. With her defenses at an all-time low, she might cave in to his expertly applied pressure.

Neither Conner nor Richard stood on the other side of the door, which wasn't much of a relief. Instead, it was the third last person she wanted to see: her mother.

"Dallas?" Marina's muffled voice penetrated the barrier. "Let me in. I know you're home. I saw your car."

Busted, and without any other options, she opened the door. The look of sorrow on her mother's face made Dallas regret leaving that voice mail message about her and Conner's argument.

She refused to call it a breakup, since technically they'd been dating less than two weeks—if she counted the charity event.

Hardly worth the flood of tears she'd been shedding practically nonstop in the two days since he'd walked out of her house and, very likely, out of her life.

Pregnancy hormones. That had to be the reason. Dallas wasn't normally so emotional.

"Oh, my darling." Marina stepped inside, shut the door and opened her arms.

Dallas, determined to be strong and remain in control, fell apart the moment her mother said, "There, there," and stroked her hair.

Having a shoulder to cry on was definitely better than crying alone.

"It's going to be okay."

"I know." Sniffing, Dallas pulled away and plucked a fresh tissue from the supply in her bathrobe pocket. "It's not like we were in love or anything."

Marina looked aghast. "Of course you were in love. Still are. Anyone can see it."

Dallas's tears flowed anew.

This simply had to stop.

"Maybe a little in love," she admitted in a tiny voice.

"Come on." Her mother propelled her to the couch. "Sit. I'll make us some herbal tea."

"You don't have to do that."

"I want to."

"It's all ri—"

"Let me do this, darling. For both of us."

Dallas nodded and worked on composing herself while her mother fussed in the kitchen. When she returned a few minutes later, bearing two steaming mugs of tea, Dallas felt marginally better.

Would she be as good a parent to her own child as Marina was to her? Instinctively know what her child needed even when he or she didn't?

"What are those?" Marina asked as she sat beside Dallas on the couch.

"Proofs. For an ad. FedEx delivered them today."

Her mom set her mug on the coffee table before picking up the ad proofs with Conner on the mountaintop. "They're good. You're becoming very skilled."

"Thanks," Dallas muttered around her mug, wishing the warmth could somehow reach her chilled heart.

"He is indeed a handsome man."

He was. She remembered seeing their reflection in the mirrored hallway at the Phoenician, and thinking how attractive he was. How striking a couple they made.

"Want to tell me what happened?" her mother asked gently. "More than just 'I made a mistake,' which is all I got from that garbled message you left."

"I did make a mistake. I told him I'd talk with my associates at the AAWA. See if they were hiring and put in a good word for him."

"Ah." Marina nodded in understanding.

"'Ah?' What's so wrong with that? I was trying to help."

"Yes, you were."

"I hear a silent 'but' at the end of that."

"Men like Conner are proud."

"Tell me about it."

"They have a hard time accepting help from others, a harder time accepting help from a women."

"That's what he said."

"It's encrypted in their DNA. The trick we women have to learn, if we insist on loving men like them, is to help without being obvious."

"Is that what you do with Hank?"

Marina leaned back into the couch cushions, a satisfied grin on her face. "I've become so good at it he hasn't noticed for years now."

Her mother must be *really* good if Dallas hadn't noticed it, either.

"Conner thought I was helping him find a job because I'm embarrassed that he's a ranch hand."

"That's his guilt and feelings of inadequacy talking."

"Exactly what I said, though not in those words."

"It's also not entirely true." Marina squeezed Dallas's hand. "Dig deep, baby girl. Be honest with yourself. Isn't there a part of you, maybe a small part, that wishes he had a better job?"

"Yes." Fresh tears filled her eyes. "God, I'm awful."

"No, you're not. It's natural for us to want the best for our loved ones. For them to live up to their potential. It's only wrong when the reasons are selfish."

Dallas understood what her mother was saying, not that it did her any good now.

"I wish men were more like us."

Marina laughed. "Do you?"

"They don't have any problems offering us help with our careers, and think we're stupid if we turn them down because of pride."

"You're right."

"Then there are men like Hank, who don't want their wife to have a career at all."

"Dallas! How could you say such a thing?"

She exchanged a crumbled tissue for a fresh one. "Well, he made you give up sculpting."

"He did not! I sculpt."

"A few pieces a year. You're talented, Mom. You could have become famous."

"I don't know about that. But even if I could have been famous, I didn't want it."

"Yes, you did."

"No." She made sound of distress. "I don't know where you're getting all these ideas about Hank."

"You've always talked so…longingly about your art."

"Because I love it. Like you love photography. You talk longingly about that."

"But…" Dallas gave up trying to explain.

"I quit pursuing a career as an artist to raise you and Liam, be Hank's wife and teach. The three most important things in my life." Marina tucked a lock of disheveled hair behind Dallas's ear. "I have everything I've always wanted. I don't know why you thought differently."

Dallas didn't know, either.

"My fault, I suppose." Marina sighed. "I always pushed you and Liam. Somewhere along the line I must have unintentionally allowed you to assume it was because of some personal dissatisfaction."

"You weren't the one who pushed us. Hank did. All those rules of his."

Marina looked stricken. "I've really messed up."

"What are you talking about?"

"I was the one who made the rules. Hank simply enforced them."

"What?"

"I've always been such a softie where you and your brother were concerned. After your father and I divorced, I didn't want you thinking both your parents didn't love you. If it was left entirely up to me, you and Liam would have run completely wild. Hank was so much better at disciplining than me." Guilt shone brightly on her face. "I let him take over the task."

Dallas's jaw went slack. "You made the rules? Didn't let us watch TV after nine on weekdays? No date till we were sixteen? Drive until we were eighteen?"

"I've been so unfair to Hank. You, too. I see now how it's affected your relationship with him. I thought all along it was some misguided loyalty to your father." She blinked her damp eyes. "I'm the worst mother in history."

Dallas suddenly saw her years growing up with her stepfather in an entirely new light. "You are the worst mother."

Marina looked shocked, then agreed resignedly. "I am."

"And the most wonderful one." Dallas hugged her mother fiercely and kissed her soundly on the cheek.

"What's all this?"

"Can I come over tomorrow? Early. Before Hank leaves for the office."

"Of course. But why—"

"I want to apologize to him."

"Darling, you don't have to do that. Like I said, it's my fault."

Dallas wouldn't be deterred. "I'll bring him breakfast. Does he still like those whole wheat pancakes from Wild Flower Bread Company?"

"They're his favorite." Marina smiled, happy again. "He loves you, you know. In his way."

"I do know. And I suppose I love him, too. In my way."

Marina slapped her thighs with a back-to-business enthusiasm. "Now, what are we going to do about you and Conner?"

There was no point in Dallas confessing her love for him, too. As her mother had already pointed out, that was obvious.

"I owe him an apology, as well."

"You need to come up with something better than whole wheat pancakes."

She picked up the ad proofs and considered her mother's remark. "I think I've figured out just the thing."

"How long have you and I been friends?" Richard asked. "Six, seven years?"

"Something like that."

He and Conner walked down the barn aisle, with no particular destination that Conner knew of in mind.

"We've been to football games, bachelor parties, barbecues, company events, dinners at each other's house. All that and yet I've never been here."

"I don't suppose I ever invited you." He still wasn't sure why Richard had appeared out of the blue. Apparently, he was going to tell him in his own sweet time.

Conner assumed it had something to do with Dallas. She must have told Richard about them.

"I want to thank you again for helping me with Rosco and Evelyn. Things aren't perfect. But we're making strides. The department's running smoother and morale's slowly improving."

"I'm glad." Conner was, for his former employees and his former friend. The better Richard did his job, the better he could take care of Dallas and their child.

"Do all these horses belong to the Powells?" He gave the

many large heads hanging over the stall doors a strange look, as if they were alien beings.

Conner supposed they were to Richard. He wasn't the cowboy type.

The two of them were so unalike. How had they been friends?

How had Dallas cared for them both?

"About half the horses belong to clients."

"Where's that wild stallion you and Dallas are always talking about? And the—what is it? Mustang sanctuary?"

"Prince has his own quarters in the next barn over. The sanctuary's a few minutes away. At the Duvall Rodeo Arena."

Richard let his gaze wander to the neighboring barn. "Maybe you can take me to see him."

"Prince? I could, but why?"

"I don't want to wait for the book to come out." Richard's smile and joke fell flat.

Conner studied him. "What's the real reason you're here?"

"I heard you and Dallas are seeing each other. Not from her. Evelyn told me. I think she was rubbing my nose in it. Which I may have deserved,"

Conner debated telling him that, as of Wednesday, he had nothing to worry about. But decided to see where the conversation went first.

"How did Evelyn find out?"

"There was a picture of you and Dallas at an AAWA dinner. Triad put it in the corporate newsletter."

Conner remembered. Back when Dallas and Richard were engaged, she'd petitioned Triad to include the Arizona Animal Welfare Association among the charitable organizations to which they made annual donations.

There had been a lot of photographs taken at the dinner. It hadn't occurred to Conner one might appear in Triad's newsletter.

"She's not going to marry me, is she?"

The lost look on Richard's face struck a chord with Conner. He'd seen a similar look in the mirror that morning.

"I have no idea what she's going to do." At Richard's puzzled expression, he said, "We're not seeing each other. We did. Briefly. A few dates. It didn't last."

Their relationship had been much, much more than just a few dates to Conner. If he hadn't messed up, it could have been the start of a lifetime together.

Richard appeared to digest that information. Any comments he had he kept to himself.

"I wish I knew when she fell out of love with me. What I could say that would make her change her mind."

Conner's chest tightened. He didn't want Richard and Dallas together. At the same time, the man was clearly hurting.

"You've done everything right. You'll be there when she needs you. And your baby needs you."

Richard's gaze wandered to the riders practicing in the arena. Near the hay shed, Javier and another hand were loading the flatbed trailer with bales in preparation for the evening feeding.

"If I had to pick another man for her, I couldn't do better than you."

"No chance I'll be taking your place. You're that child's father."

"I'll be a good one." He squared his shoulders. "It wasn't what I wanted. Not at first. I didn't think I was ready. But I'll be okay."

Conner recalled Dallas's comment about how her life wasn't playing out in the order she'd planned.

The same could be said for all three of them.

"You'll do fine." He automatically raised an arm to give Richard's shoulder a friendly squeeze.

He let his hand drop before making contact.

Richard gave no indication he'd noticed.

"Hey, I didn't drop by to moan about myself." He withdrew a business card from his bomber jacket pocket and handed it to Conner. "An old college roommate of mine recently went to work for this outfit."

Conner read the card. Infinity Renewable Energy Systems. According to the address, they were located in northeast Phoenix. "What about him?"

"Not him. Them. They're hiring and have an opening for a production manager. I gave them your name."

"You did?"

"They need someone with experience who can hit the ground running. They have a pretty impressive product line and a solid vision of how to grow the company. He's expecting your call. Today."

Conner studied the card, not sure what to say. After Sonoran Bottling, he didn't dare get his hopes up.

"Keep in mind," Richard continued, "they're a start-up organization. The salary won't be anything near what you were earning at Triad. But if they take off, and they could—there's an expanding market for green energy systems—you'll be in on the ground floor. If it were me, I'd ask for stock options."

"Why would you do this for me? We haven't been the best of friends lately."

"For the same reason you helped me with Rosco and Evelyn."

"I didn't want them to lose their jobs."

Richard cocked his head, his eyes searching. "Really? That was all?"

It wasn't all. Deep in his heart, Conner didn't blame Richard for the loss of his job. Punishing him would have been unfair.

Considering that Richard had been under the assumption Conner and Dallas were dating, recommending Conner for a job was, well, pretty decent of him.

"Thank you." This time, Conner didn't hesitate; his hand made firm contact with Richard's shoulder.

"I've got another stop to make."

Conner nodded. "Come back again. When you have more time." The invitation was heartfelt.

Richard seemed to sense that. "I will. You can show me that wild stallion. Then maybe we can go out for beer."

"I'd like that. My treat."

"We'll celebrate your new job."

After Richard left, Conner walked to the stall holding Chiquita and her colt. Both immediately came over for a petting.

Conner pulled out his cell phone and, reading the name and number off the business card, placed the call to Richard's old roommate.

The man was pleased to hear from Conner. They spoke for almost twenty minutes, ending the call with a meeting scheduled for first thing in the morning. Conner liked what the man had to say, and had the impression they could work well together.

He would owe Richard a depth of gratitude if he got the job.

What would Dallas think?

She'd probably tell him what she'd been saying all along—it wasn't *what* Conner knew that mattered but *who*. In this case, Richard. Go figure.

During the entire phone call, Conner had stood at the stall, his free hand stroking the colt.

"Maybe I will get to keep you, after all. Would you like that?"

The colt answered by nibbling his fingers.

Conner realized that, in all probability, this little guy would be the last wild horse ever to be born in Mustang Valley.

"Principito. Little Prince. That's what I'm going to call you."

The colt snorted.

"Too long? How 'bout Pito for short?"

With that, the colt officially became Conner's.

He thought of going in search of Gavin, to tell him about the interview with Infinity. He didn't. He'd wait until he had a job offer in hand.

Then what? Tell Dallas?

For all he knew, she didn't want to see him again. Ever.

To finally land the kind of job he'd been hoping for after seven long months, and not have her to share it with, didn't seem fair.

Of course, getting a new job would be a good excuse to call her.

Chapter Sixteen

Conner's truck wasn't parked by his apartment. Dallas assured herself there was no reason to assume she'd missed him. He often used his truck for chores around the ranch. As she was driving to the parking area, she noticed Gavin and Sage at the arena fence, watching a young woman riding a tall, leggy black horse. Gavin appeared to be giving her instructions.

They turned to look as Dallas pulled to a stop and got out of her car. It was then she noticed Sage was carrying Milo, snuggled against her in a baby wrap. As Dallas approached, his arms and legs started flailing. She chose to think he was excited to see her. She was certainly excited to see him.

"How are you?" Sage greeted Dallas with a warm hug. Milo squawked, annoyed at being squished between the two women, one who insisted on pinching his chin.

Dallas got a kiss on the cheek from Gavin—a you're-one-of-the-family kind of kiss.

Nice.

"What brings you here?" he asked. "Not that we aren't glad to see you."

"I have something for Conner."

"Conner?" Sage's brows rose quizzically.

"The agency sent me proofs of the ad. The one with his picture. I made copies for him. Thought he might want them." She pulled a proof out of the manila envelope.

"Wow!" Sage studied it admiringly. "He'll definitely like this."

Gavin offered similar praise.

Dallas looked at the proof with fresh eyes. It *was* praiseworthy. Her best yet. Being a respected documentary photographer really wasn't such a far-fetched dream.

Would she give up the chance of becoming one for a life with Conner, as her mother had done with Hank?

No. Because she wouldn't have to. Conner would always support and encourage her. The same way she needed to support and encourage his dreams—and not just because his success was a positive reflection on her.

"Is he here?" She scanned the immediate area.

"Not at the moment."

She felt her face fall. "I should have called first."

"He's at the mustang sanctuary," Gavin said. "Settling in a new arrival."

Doubts promptly assailed her. "I don't want to bother him if he's working. I can come back later."

"You won't be bothering him." Sage's smile reached her eyes. "Trust me."

They must not have heard. "We had a…disagreement the other day."

"We know. He told us." Gavin's tone was sympathetic.

Okay, they had heard.

"I'm sorry." Sage's smile turned sad.

Even Milo commiserated by suddenly whining.

"Why don't you drive out to the sanctuary? I'm sure he'll be glad to see you."

Dallas did want to apologize. Tell Conner what a fool she'd been. Even if nothing came of it, at least she'd sleep better at night.

"What if he isn't glad to see me?"

"He misses you, too."

Did he? Was he also putting up a good front just for show?

"I guess I will drive by the sanctuary. To drop off the proofs," she clarified, when Sage and Gavin exchanged knowing glances.

Her Prius kicked up a cloud of dust as she maneuvered it along the dirt road. The pastures where the mustangs resided came into view, Conner's truck a small white dot in the distance.

Her nerves started tingling as she scanned the area for any sign of him. She didn't see him until she got closer. He was in the pasture, the mustangs clustered around him like adoring fans. Except for one, a shaggy, nondescript mare who warily kept her distance.

The new addition, Dallas concluded.

Soon enough, the mare would learn to trust Conner.

As Dallas did. Enough to place her future and that of her child's alongside his. If he'd still have her after the way she'd let him down. She would wait if necessary. For as long as it took.

With a gentle pat to the many heads surrounding him, he strode toward the gate. He must have recognized her car long before she emerged, manila envelope in hand. What was he thinking? Was his heart beating a mile a minute like hers, or were hurt and anger ruling his emotions?

"Hi." The carefully guarded expression on his face revealed nothing.

"I, um…Sage and Gavin said it was okay. I'm not disturbing you, am I?"

"Just playing cowboy."

"You don't play at it, Conner. You're talented. You have every reason to be proud of your accomplishments."

A small smile played at the corners of his mouth. "I'm glad you're here."

"You are?" Were his reasons the same as hers?

"Gavin got a call this morning from the Scottsdale police."

"They found the person who shot the mare!"

"He came forward."

Dallas was glad—and furious. "I hope they throw the book at him. He deserves it."

"Actually, according to the officer who called, he'll probably only be charged with a misdemeanor."

"That's all?"

"He claimed it was an accident. And there are no witnesses."

"Accident, my foot!"

"He did come forward. He could have kept quiet."

"Hmm." She wasn't satisfied.

"He also offered to make a donation to the mustang sanctuary."

Dallas was somewhat mollified when Conner named the amount. "Still, it wasn't right. He should have reported shooting the mare when it happened."

"Yeah, she was injured. But she and Pito are fine now. And a lot of positive attention came from all the media coverage."

"True." Something Conner had said suddenly occurred to Dallas. "Pito? Is that what you named the colt?"

"It's short for *Principito*."

"Little Prince. I like it."

"By the way—" his smile grew "—what brings you by?"

"This." Dallas held out the envelope.

Conner took it and removed one print, then another. "Not what I expected."

"You don't like them?" Her spirits sank.

"I do. They're great. I just don't see myself as an advertisement for a car dealership."

"Exploring the Southwest in your brand-new truck," she explained. "Wide-open spaces. Modern-day cowboy."

"If you say so."

"It's a gimmick. A way to entice customers to the dealership."

"And an effective one. I think I'll buy a new truck from this place. Maybe they'll give me a smoking deal."

"Sure. I can see you in one." Someday. When he was back on his feet financially. "But I like your old truck. It has character. Been though some tough times and keeps running."

Like its owner.

"Can't continue driving this junker to my new job."

"New job?"

His small smile transformed into a full-blown grin. "Infinity Renewable Energy Systems. I start on Monday."

"When... What... How long have you known?"

"I interviewed with them this morning. They offered me the position on the spot. You're the first person I've told. I wanted a little time to myself to let it sink in."

Before she quite realized what had happened, she was in his arms.

He caught her, swinging her off her feet. They both laughed.

"I'm so happy for you." As he set her down, she cradled his face in her hands and kissed him full on the mouth. "Did you find the job online?"

"Richard told me about it."

"Richard? No way!"

"He came by to see me yesterday. We talked. Things between us are better."

"I can't believe he helped you land a job."

"Sure you can. He's not a bad guy."

"He's not. Actually, he's a sweetheart, and I'm lucky to have him for my baby's father."

Conner filled her in on the details about the job. There was more potential than immediate reward, but it was perfect for him.

"I'll have to work a lot of hours the first year or two."

"Being afraid of hard work isn't one of your faults."

"I won't have as much time for the horses."

"Are you okay with that?"

"I am. I have other interests closer to home."

"Such as?"

His reply was to take her in his arms again and kiss her senseless.

Oh, my goodness!

She needed several seconds afterward to catch her breath. "I'm sorry about the other day. I wasn't—"

"Shut up."

"What?"

"We both made mistakes. Said things we shouldn't have, out of anger and hurt. It happens with couples. We'll talk it out, learn from it and move on. Then we'll be better, stronger, more in love than we were before."

"Are we in love?" She was and had been since the dinner with Sage and Gavin, when he'd tenderly held Milo.

"Crazy. Wildly. Enough in love that I'm not letting you leave here without agreeing to marry me."

"M-marry you?"

"I've never proposed before. Should I get on bended knee?" He started to lower himself.

"Stop!" She tugged him to his feet.

"You're turning me down?" He looked devastated.

"No. I mean yes, I will marry you." Her words came out in a jumbled rush. "Just don't go down on one knee."

"What should I do?"

"Kiss me. Buy me a ring. Take my parents to dinner and tell them over champagne."

"I think I can handle all that."

"I do have one request." She turned pleading eyes on him. "Make time for the horses. You're a smart and gifted businessman. But you're also a cowboy, with traditional values and beliefs. That's exactly the kind of role model I want for my child. *Our* child."

"Richard's the father."

"And you'll be the stepfather. There every day helping me. Whether I like admitting it or not, Hank played a big role in shaping me into the person I am."

"Remind me to thank him."

"You can. At the wedding, when he walks me down the aisle."

Conner gave her that kiss she'd asked for. "Marry me, Dallas. Love me always."

"Yes to both. Forever and ever."

They drove back to Powell Ranch in Conner's old truck, to share the news with their friends. Dallas was definitely going to talk him into keeping it. If anything, as a reminder of where'd they been and how far they'd come.

It had taken her a while, but she finally understood the lesson her mother had tried to teach her. Everyone must choose their own path to happiness, not the one others think they should.

Dallas was utterly certain her path to happiness included Conner, their respective careers and the family they would create together.

Epilogue

Five months later

Conner stood outside Dallas's hospital door, holding a bouquet of freshly cut flowers. He'd been about to go in, and hesitated when he spotted Richard standing over the bassinet and gazing fondly at his daughter, Grace Marina. She was named for both her grandmothers, who'd been there for the birth and only left within the past hour.

Conner thought Richard had left, too.

He didn't barge in. Instead he gave Richard and Dallas a few minutes of privacy. Conner would have to get used to that. They were Grace's parents and, as such, there'd be times when Conner would have to watch silently from the sidelines.

He was okay with that. Just as Richard would be okay watching silently from the sidelines when it came to Conner and Dallas.

They'd done pretty well so far, handling potentially awkward and difficult situations with calm and reason. Such as the holidays, Conner and Dallas's wedding two months ago and Grace's birth late last night. When Conner would have remained outside in the waiting room, Richard had agreed to Dallas's request that he be allowed to stay during the delivery.

Conner had held her hand. It was Richard, however, who got to hold baby Grace first, after Dallas.

Next time, when Conner and Dallas gave Grace a younger brother or sister, he would hold Dallas's hand *and* the baby.

"Hey, come on in."

He looked up to find Richard smiling foolishly—like a man who'd just become a father for the first time—and motioning him in the room.

Dallas reached out a hand. When he neared the bed, she drew him down for a light peck on the lips. "Baby's sleeping. Mommy wants to sleep, too."

None of them had rested more than a few hours after the 1:27 a.m. birth. Conner's Z's were courtesy of the painfully uncomfortable chair beside Dallas's bed.

"Better hurry," he told her. "I think you're being released in a few hours."

"Are these for me?" She took the flowers. "They're lovely."

"I'm heading home." Richard stretched and yawned. "Call me if you need anything." He came over and kissed Dallas on the forehead.

"I will. Thank you, Richard."

There was affection in their voices, that of two friends and two people committed to being wonderful parents to their daughter.

"Do you mind if I stop by tomorrow after work to visit Gracie? I won't stay long."

"That would be fine."

"I'll bring dinner if you can stand eating takeout." Richard extended his hand to Conner.

They weren't going to be one big, happy family. But they would manage well enough.

After Richard left, Conner went over to the bassinet and took in his fill of sleeping Grace. Unable to resist, he slipped his index finger into her tiny, delicate hand and was rewarded with a light squeeze.

"Sleep tight, beautiful girl."

She was beautiful, a combination of the best traits from both her parents.

Conner would have some influence on her, too. If he had anything to say about it, she'd grow up to be the roughest, toughest cowgirl in Mustang Valley. About the time she was ready for her first horse, Pito would be trained and gentled.

The tradition of wild mustangs and the cowfolk who rode them would continue for another generation.

He returned to the bed. Dallas was almost asleep, her eyelids drifting shut, the bouquet of flowers in her hand.

There were several other floral arrangements in the room, one from Infinity. Conner's job had turned out to be harder than he'd anticipated, and came with demanding hours.

He loved every minute and couldn't wait to go to work in the mornings.

The only thing he loved more was coming home in the evenings to Dallas.

He bent and nuzzled her cheek. "I love you."

She mumbled her love in return before drifting off again.

Conner thought about lying down next to her, but then little Gracie started making anxious mewling sounds. He went over and instinctively rested a hand on her tummy to comfort her. She didn't stop.

Not wanting the cries to wake Dallas, Conner lifted Grace out of the bassinet, adjusted her blanket and held her against his chest. "Shhh."

"Bring her here," Dallas said sleepily, and set the flowers on the nightstand.

She'd woken up anyway, despite his efforts. He supposed

mothers were keenly attuned to their babies' every noise and movement. Especially new ones.

Carrying Grace, he laid her in Dallas's outstretched arms. She scooted over and patted the mattress beside her.

While she held their baby, Conner held her—and kept holding her long after she fell asleep.

* * * * *

COMING NEXT MONTH
from Harlequin® American Romance®

AVAILABLE APRIL 2, 2013

#1445 HIS CALLAHAN BRIDE'S BABY
Callahan Cowboys
Tina Leonard
Sweet and independent Taylor Waters won't accept Falcon Callahan's marriage proposal. But he's determined to win Diablo's best girl, even when the whole town puts him to the test!

#1446 HER COWBOY DILEMMA
Coffee Creek, Montana
C.J. Carmichael
Prodigal daughter Cassidy Lambert is home—temporarily—to help out at the family ranch. But seeing local vet Dan Farley again is making her question her decision to live in the big city.

#1447 NO ORDINARY COWBOY
Rodeo Rebels
Marin Thomas
Lucy Durango needs Tony Bravo to teach her how to ride bulls. Tony reluctantly agrees, and he'll do what he can to keep her safe. Even if her daddy warns him to stay away....

#1448 THE RANCHER AND THE VET
Fatherhood
Julie Benson
Reed Montgomery returns to the family ranch in Colorado to care for his fourteen-year-old niece, Jess. There Reed must face his difficult past, his cowboy roots and Avery McAlister, the girl he loved and left.

You can find more information on upcoming Harlequin® titles, free excerpts and more at www.Harlequin.com.

HARCNM0313

REQUEST YOUR FREE BOOKS!
2 FREE NOVELS PLUS 2 *FREE GIFTS!*

HARLEQUIN®

American ★ Romance®

LOVE, HOME & HAPPINESS

YES! Please send me 2 FREE Harlequin® American Romance® novels and my 2 FREE gifts (gifts are worth about $10). After receiving them, if I don't wish to receive any more books, I can return the shipping statement marked "cancel." If I don't cancel, I will receive 4 brand-new novels every month and be billed just $4.49 per book in the U.S. or $5.24 per book in Canada. That's a savings of at least 14% off the cover price! It's quite a bargain! Shipping and handling is just 50¢ per book in the U.S. and 75¢ per book in Canada.* I understand that accepting the 2 free books and gifts places me under no obligation to buy anything. I can always return a shipment and cancel at any time. Even if I never buy another book, the two free books and gifts are mine to keep forever.

154/354 HDN FVPK

Name _____ (PLEASE PRINT) _____

Address _____ Apt. # _____

City _____ State/Prov. _____ Zip/Postal Code _____

Signature (if under 18, a parent or guardian must sign)

Mail to the **Harlequin®** Reader Service:
IN U.S.A.: P.O. Box 1867, Buffalo, NY 14240-1867
IN CANADA: P.O. Box 609, Fort Erie, Ontario L2A 5X3

Want to try two free books from another line?
Call 1-800-873-8635 or visit www.ReaderService.com.

* Terms and prices subject to change without notice. Prices do not include applicable taxes. Sales tax applicable in N.Y. Canadian residents will be charged applicable taxes. Offer not valid in Quebec. This offer is limited to one order per household. Not valid for current subscribers to Harlequin American Romance books. All orders subject to credit approval. Credit or debit balances in a customer's account(s) may be offset by any other outstanding balance owed by or to the customer. Please allow 4 to 6 weeks for delivery. Offer available while quantities last.

Your Privacy—The Harlequin® Reader Service is committed to protecting your privacy. Our Privacy Policy is available online at www.ReaderService.com or upon request from the Harlequin Reader Service.

We make a portion of our mailing list available to reputable third parties that offer products we believe may interest you. If you prefer that we not exchange your name with third parties, or if you wish to clarify or modify your communication preferences, please visit us at www.ReaderService.com/consumerchoice or write to us at Harlequin Reader Service Preference Service, P.O. Box 9062, Buffalo, NY 14269. Include your complete name and address.

HAR13

The **CALLAHAN COWBOY** *series continues with*
Tina Leonard's HIS CALLAHAN BRIDE'S BABY.

Falcon has his work cut out for him trying to convince
Taylor to be his wife—but if his proposal doesn't work,
he'll lose his ranch land to his siblings!

Taylor Waters was one of Diablo's "best" girls. She had a reputation for being wild at heart. Untamable. Men threw themselves at her feet and she walked all over them with a sweet-natured smile.

Falcon Chacon Callahan studied the well-built brunette behind the counter of Banger's Bait and Tackle diner. He'd talked the owner, Jillian, into selling him one last beer, even though the diner usually closed at the stroke of midnight on the weekends. It was his Saturday night off from Rancho Diablo, and he hadn't wanted to do anything but relax and consider what he was going to do with his life once his job at the ranch was over.

Taylor was more of an immediate interest. She smiled that cute pixie smile at him and Falcon sipped his beer, deciding on a whim—some might call it a hunch—to toss his heart into the Taylor tizzy. "I need a wife," he said.

"So I hear. So we all hear." She came and sat on the bar stool next to him. "You'll get it figured out eventually, Falcon."

"Marry me, Taylor."

"I know you're not drunk enough to propose, Falcon. You're just crazy, like we've always heard." She smiled so adorably, all of the sting fled her words. In fact, she was so cute about her opinion that Falcon felt his chest expand.

"I leave crazy to my brothers. My sister is the wild and crazy one. Me, I'm somewhere on the other side of the spectrum." He leaned over and kissed her lightly on the lips. Falcon grinned. "What's your answer, cupcake?"

"You're not serious." Taylor shook her head. "I've known you for over a year. Of all the Callahans, you're the one the town's got odds on being last to the altar." She got up and sashayed to the register. His eyes followed her movements hungrily. "A girl would be a fool to fall for you, Falcon Callahan."

That did not sound like a *yes*.

But Falcon is a cowboy who always gets his way! Watch for his story coming in April 2013, only from Harlequin® American Romance®.

HAREXP0413

C.J. CARMICHAEL

brings readers another story from

Cassidy Lambert has dreams of a big-city life, but when an outbreak of strangles puts the family ranch under quarantine, she steps in to help before it spreads from the family's riding horses to the quarter horse breeding stock. With the chance to keep her daughter for a little longer, ranch matriarch Olive Lambert is seizing the opportunity to match her daughter with the local vet, Dan Farley.

Cassidy thinks she knows what she wants from life—but suddenly nothing feels right without Dan.

Her Cowboy Dilemma

**Available from Harlequin® American Romance®
April 2, 2013!**

www.Harlequin.com

HAR75450